"We need to come up with a plan for tomorrow," Booker said.

"Tomorrow?" Anita repeated. "I want to go look for my brother now. He might be hurt, or worse."

"No."

"No? Why not? I know you're mad at me, Booker, but don't take it out on my brother."

He met her intense brown eyes. "We can't go there at night, not without prior planning. It's too dangerous. Your brother wouldn't want you to do a fool thing like that. I'll take you in the morning."

She blinked. "Why would you do that?"

Yeah, why would you do that, Booker? He gritted his teeth. *Because I'm completely insane,* he wanted to tell her. *Out of my mind to get involved with you again when the smallest memory of you still makes me crazy.* He understood the anger she kindled in him, the hurt.

What he couldn't wrap his mind around was the strong need that rose in his gut, the need to protect her, in spite of everything.

Books by Dana Mentink

Love Inspired Suspense

Killer Cargo
Flashover
Race to Rescue

DANA MENTINK

lives in California with her family. Dana and her husband met doing a dinner theater production of *The Velveteen Rabbit*. In college, she competed in national speech and debate tournaments. Besides writing novels, Dana taste-tests for the National Food Lab and freelances for a local newspaper. In addition to her work with Steeple Hill Books, she writes cozy mysteries for Barbour Books. Dana loves feedback from her readers. Contact her at www.danamentink.com.

RACE *to* RESCUE

DANA MENTINK

Steeple
Hill®

Published by Steeple Hill Books™

STEEPLE HILL BOOKS

Steeple
Hill®

Recycling programs
for this product may
not exist in your area.

ISBN-13: 978-0-373-44355-0

RACE TO RESCUE

www.SteepleHill.com

Printed in U.S.A.

And we know that in all things God works for the good of those who love him, who have been called according to His purpose.

—*Romans* 8:28

To the Lord for setting my feet on this journey and Penny Warner for helping me along the way.

ONE

There's nothing wrong, she told herself. There's a logical explanation.

Anita made an effort to put the worry about her brother away as the darkness closed around her in a moist fist. She took the thermal imaging binoculars from her backpack and tried to find a more comfortable position on the small mat. But no matter how she settled her slender frame, the rock fragments seemed to find her. The whine of mosquitoes sounded constantly in her ears.

Focus on the job, Anita. Do what you've waited years to do. She was a hundred yards away from the most exciting moment of her career. Buried deep in this forest in the Seychelles Islands was something she had been hoping to see for a decade.

In spite of the excitement, the worry about her brother crept back. They always connected somehow on July 15, the anniversary of the accident that took their parents' lives. Even if they were half a world apart, Drew managed an e-mail or a quick text message. It was a pact they'd made and kept faithfully.

Until now.

She mentally calculated the date in the States again. No, she hadn't made a mistake. It was now July 17, and still no word from her brother. She took a deep breath to release the knots in her stomach as she eyed the sun, sinking slowly into the Indian Ocean in a swirl of vibrant crimson. *Pay attention, Anita. Another fifteen minutes, maybe, and they'll be here.*

The tiny island was bisected by a ridge of mountain. The upper region where she was camped was forested and rugged, which saved it from the ravages of residential and agricultural use. Palms rustled in the cool ocean breeze.

Anita swatted at a mosquito that buzzed her ear. She pulled up her long, kinky brown hair and applied another squirt of bug repellent to her neck. Her job still felt surreal to her. She relished the chance to be in a corner of the world that few people saw, to have an opportunity to document one of the ten most endangered species in the world, a species that might be brought back from the brink of extinction with her help.

The sun disappeared and the sky changed to a soft gray. Anita readied her binoculars and trained them on the mouth of the cave. When the animals were dormant yesterday, she'd quietly hacked away the kudzu vine that threatened to choke access to the cave. Her hands still ached from the effort.

After a few more moments of silence, there came a sound like the rush of an angry stream. Anita had just enough time to ready the video camera as the sheath-tailed bats surged out of the cave mouth. They rose as a large, black shadow against the sky, chittering as they flew out in search of insects. She craned her head to watch their progress, counting as quickly as she could.

Then the cloud vanished as the bats disappeared into the night.

Anita leaned back on her mat, her skin still prickled in goose bumps. Unbelievably, the precious bats were alive and healthy here, and she felt more determined than ever to see that this tiny colony survived in the face of a world that seemed equally determined to stamp them out.

She covered her mouth with a mask to filter out the ammonia gases that enveloped the bats' home, and stole into the cave to collect guano samples and photograph the roost. Her fingers shook as she worked. There would be no way to undo the damage if the bats returned and were spooked by a human presence. The cave was damp and still. Piles of droppings collected in heaps upon the floor. It took her no more than ten minutes before she hurried out again, panting and damp with sweat.

She settled down on her mat to wait for the bats' return, readying an infrared camera this time. The piece of equipment brought Drew to her mind in a sudden rush of worry. He would laugh his head off to see Anita taking pictures. He always said people should give her the camera only if they wanted a close-up of her thumbs. She checked her PDA again, but there was still nothing from him.

Maybe he couldn't get a message through to her remote location. Her comfort was fleeting. She'd been able to call his Arizona apartment several times, and he hadn't answered. None of her e-mails had gotten a response, either.

Anita's mind traveled back to the hot, arid desert, where her brother was a photographer for the prestigious *Wild World Magazine.* Someone else surfaced in her thoughts: a big man with vibrant blue eyes and a strong chin. She tried to shake his handsome face from her mind.

Forget it, Anita. You did what you had to do. Booker will see that someday.

Deep down she knew she was fooling herself. He'd never forgive her, though she was certain she'd done the right thing when *Wild World's* owner, Cyrus Leeman, pointed her to the colony of endangered bats on Booker's property. He couldn't be allowed to put them at risk, and she'd made sure he didn't have the chance.

But why did she feel so bad about the look of betrayal on his face when he'd found out?

Had her face borne the same expression when Jack, the love of her life, had cracked her world apart? She took a deep breath. Her actions had nothing to do with love, she reminded herself sternly. Her feelings for Booker had been a mistake, and relationships sometimes had to be sacrificed for the greater good. They'd dated for months, spent every free moment together until that wonderful, awful moment he'd told her he loved her. It still made her breath catch to recall it.

Buried in thought, she lost track of time. She was relieved when an hour or so later, the *whoosh* of wings announced the return of the bat colony. Her fingers took over, taking pictures, swiveling the camera from side to side until the swell of the winged tide was over. She packed up her gear and headed down the gravel path toward camp when her satellite phone vibrated. Frowning, she looked at the screen. The number was familiar, starting her heart into a quick staccato. "Drew?"

The voice on the other end was faint, raspy. "Ani."

There was only one person who would dare call her Ani. She pressed the phone closer to her ear and listened to her brother's irregular gasps. "What's wrong? You sound out of breath."

There was a delay before he answered. "Need your help."

She felt a stir of fear as she struggled to hear him through the bad connection. Drew didn't need help for anything. He was ever the bullheaded, larger-than-life brother who shot first and aimed later. "Tell me."

His voice faded in and out. "…trouble."

She felt a stab of alarm. "I can't hear you. Tell me again. Where are you?"

"Please…gotten myself in too deep this time."

Her throat constricted. "What happened? Are you still in Arizona?"

"Yeah, I've been…" Dead space swallowed up his words. "You've gotta help me, Ani."

"I can't hear you. It's a bad connection. Are you hurt? Do you need the police?"

Drew managed one more word before the phone clicked off.

Anita stood stock-still, her body taut. Frantically she redialed Drew's number and got an "out of service" message for her trouble. If his words hadn't scared her enough, the desperate tone of his voice had. He needed her help to escape from something, something deadly.

She had to go; she had to find him.

His final word tumbled over and over in her ears.

Murder.

The harsh Arizona sunlight beat down on Booker Scott as he wrenched the barbed wire back into place. Second time this week it'd been cut. He knew exactly who was responsible, and he knew they'd be back, with more help and more firepower. They were checking things out, seeing if his property offered the necessary amenities. Ace reached a paw up to scratch under his collar, his sturdy German shepherd body parked in the shade of the pickup.

"They're getting bolder, Ace." He wondered if they were watching him at that moment from some concealed spot in the rugged side of the distant gorge. But even more menacing than the trespassers on his property were the bankers, looking for their pound of flesh. He'd take guns over bankers any day.

He fought against the desperate feeling that rose in his gut. *It's still my land for a while longer.* His eyes followed the sun-parched ground, speckled with boulders bearing resurrection moss, until it folded into the steep gorge on the western periphery of the property. The black mouth of Mesquite Cave was almost invisible, tucked into the shadow of the massive rock that overshadowed it.

It was all there, the key to saving his ranch and his father. Right there, but locked away from him as surely as if it was chained in a steel vault somewhere. Thanks to Cyrus Leeman and his beautiful helper, Anita Teel. He allowed his mind to picture her for only a moment. Long hair, brown eyes, determined chin, full lips that left an indelible imprint on his.

"Trabajo?"

He whirled around to face the small man with the battered straw hat. He knew the guy's name was Diego.

"Trabajo?" Diego repeated, wiping the sweat from his forehead.

Work? Booker almost laughed. How could he possibly pay to have someone else work his property when he could hardly afford to keep it going now? "No, man. Sorry."

Diego nodded and turned to shuffle off.

Booker stopped him. "Here." He tossed Diego a cold water bottle from the small cooler he'd brought along.

The man caught the bottle and tipped his hat. *"Gracias."*

Booker nodded back, threw his toolbox in the back of the pickup and fired the engine to life. Ace jumped into the back, and they headed into town.

He didn't expect to see Cyrus Leeman chatting with the Border Patrol agent Tony Rogelio in front of the bank as he eased his truck to the curb. Rogelio gave him a nod and drove away in his own vehicle. Once again, Booker wondered if the agent was a man to be trusted. He tamped down the worry and started across the sun-baked sidewalk.

Ace dutifully followed Booker out of the truck and stood in a shaded spot.

Leeman cocked his head in between sips of water from a bottle. "Mr. Scott."

Booker wondered why the wiry man didn't ever seem to sweat, not even on the bald spot that gleamed in the sunlight. He nodded and continued past until Leeman stopped him.

"How are things going on the ranch? Heard you sold off some of your stock and two horses."

Booker turned to face him. "Not your business."

Leeman smiled, showing perfectly straight teeth. "Just being neighborly."

"Neighborly?" Booker felt his self-control snap. "You want my property and you'll do whatever it takes to get it. Don't need neighbors like that." The dog picked up on the tension in his owner's voice. He straightened, ears stiff and body tense.

Leeman shot the animal a wary look and capped the water bottle. "Is your dog friendly?"

"Most of the time, but he's a real good judge of character."

Ace kept intense eyes trained on Leeman.

He shrugged. "Now really, Scott. You are paranoid. Why would I want that useless piece of land? There's no easy water access. Can't even mine on it, anyway."

Booker clenched his fists to keep from punching Leeman in the gut. "You made sure of that, didn't you?"

He shrugged. "Environmental protection isn't my main concern. That was your girlfriend's bailiwick."

"Not my girlfriend and again, not your business." He'd thought she was his girlfriend, but he'd been wrong, so wrong.

"How are those bats, anyway? Keeping a good watch over your opal mine?"

Booker straightened his baseball cap, buying a moment to steady himself. "You work hard to be that obnoxious or does it come natural?"

Leeman laughed. "Miss Teel's article about your bats was well-received. I believe her research team was given a handsome grant." He looked casually away for a moment. "She's coming to town, you know."

He struggled to take it in. Anita was coming back? The anger and bitter disappointment flared as intensely as it had four months earlier, when he discovered who she really was. He kept his face controlled in spite of the feelings that coursed through him like a swiftly moving stream. With every ounce of remaining control, Booker turned away from Leeman.

"Stay, Ace," he told the dog, and pushed through the bank doors.

Leeman was goading him. Anita had no reason to come back to Rockridge. She'd done her work, saved the world and left his heart in the dirt.

He shot a look back at Leeman, who still had the remnants of a smile on his face as he backed away from the dog. Anita wouldn't come back. His heart seemed to have developed an unsteady rhythm.

Would she?

* * *

The oppressive desert heat pressed down on Anita as she neared Rockridge in the battle-scarred Dodge she'd rented. It seemed hostile already, this place that hid her brother somewhere, in some sizzling corner. From the airport, she'd placed one frantic phone call to *Wild World Magazine*. The secretary confirmed Drew hadn't been heard from in several days. The second phone call went to the police. Their professional coolness infuriated her as it had when she'd called the first time from the Seychelles. This was her brother they referred to with such detachment. She made arrangements to meet with them as soon as she arrived.

The road reflected the summer heat back at her in angry waves. The Dodge seemed to feel it too: the engine rattled and coughed, causing her to slow to a crawl several times.

Her stomach finally convinced her to pull into a dust-covered diner. She ordered a sandwich to go and waited while they prepared it. As she collected the bag and paid, she noticed a truck pull up by the side of her rental. The driver, whose face was concealed by sunglasses and a baseball cap, peered in the side window.

Anita held her breath and watched him from the restaurant. Why was he so interested in a dented old Dodge? She stood frozen with indecision. Should she go ask the stranger what he was after? Drew's terrified words came back to her. Her brother was involved in something bad, and for some reason he hadn't shared any info with the police. Was this nosy stranger linked to his disappearance? Or was she sinking into paranoia? There was only one way to find out. Anita took a deep breath and pushed through the door.

The person in the truck turned a quick look in her direction and immediately drove off.

She tried to shake off the fear. You're a stranger in a small town, Anita, she told herself. You're a curiosity, like a new animal at the zoo.

But not a complete stranger, she reminded herself. There were at least a handful of people who remembered her last visit, and it was possible that some of them would just as soon not see her roll into their town again. Especially a certain rugged rancher.

She checked the rearview mirror as she pulled out onto the highway.

The intense sunlight made the passing landscape luminous, sprinkled only sparsely with vegetation. It brought her back to the spring study she'd done here, tracking the lesser long-nosed bats on their travels through the nectar corridor, the thousand-mile path of cactus and agave plants that stretched from Mexico to Arizona.

It never ceased to amaze her how God caused the plants to bloom in sequence from south to north, providing an enticing path for the bats and a winged platoon of pollinators. Back then the desert had seemed like some sort of Elysian field, made even sweeter because of her own attraction to Booker. Now, with her brother lost in the wide panorama and Booker out of her life for good, the air vibrated with a vague sense of threat. She'd tried calling Drew's apartment several more times with no result.

By the time she made it to the Rockridge Police Department it was late afternoon and her clothes were wrinkled and sweaty. Stealing a look in the cracked rearview mirror, she decided she looked more like a high school kid than a confident adult. She pulled her uncooperative kinks into a knot at the back of her head and applied some lipstick. There was nothing she could do about the smudge of fatigue under her brown eyes.

Her efforts yielded a slight improvement. She was a world-class researcher, a woman of science, and the police would take her seriously if it killed her.

I'll make them.

Sergeant Williams sat in a chair and dutifully typed out Anita's comments. The miniscule squad room was dank, the air conditioner unable to keep up with the relentless heat from the bank of windows that looked out on a series of warehouses. "What did he say when he called?"

"Like I told you on the phone, he said something about trouble and murder. The magazine he works for told me he hasn't been there in four days. There's no answer at his apartment, and the super says he hasn't been there, either."

Williams lifted a heavy eyebrow. She rubbed a finger along her chin, glossy and black as the cold mug of coffee that sat at her elbow. "I called her, too. She says his rent is due. Not the first time he's been late paying it."

Anita stiffened. "What is that supposed to mean?"

"Just an observation. Perhaps the situation isn't as dire as it appears. He's disappeared before, around the time the rent was due. I spoke to the magazine, as well, to…" She consulted a notepad. "To the owner, a guy named Cyrus Leeman. He says your brother is a bit on the unreliable side. This is not the first time he's been a no-show at work."

This surprised her. Leeman didn't say a word against Drew the last time they'd met. Anita felt a fire building in her chest. "My brother is in trouble, Sergeant. He was terrified when he called me. I don't care what his past history is."

"We've got to take past history into account when a missing persons report is filed, Ms. Teel. It doesn't mean we won't look for your brother."

She slammed her purse on the desk. "Listen, I flew here straight from the Seychelles Islands."

The officer folded her arms. "Long trip."

"Yes." Her tone was icy. "I interrupted critical research to come and find my brother. Do you think I would have done that if I didn't fear for his life? My work is very important." As soon as she said it, the arrogant tone of her own words struck her, but she was too caught up in the anger to give it much heed.

Williams leaned forward, her tone level, eyes burning. "Thank you for filling me in on your status. You see this folder here?" She stabbed a thick finger at the bulging manila sleeve. "This here folder is filled with important people just like you, who need this tiny police department to help them. Your request will be added to theirs. You will be given the same attention and services that they will receive. We do our absolute best for anyone, no matter how important they are, or aren't."

Anita clamped her mouth together, trying to figure out how to undo the damage.

Williams handed her a card. "I will continue to check into it. Here is my card and the number for the Department of Homeland Security. They manage the Border Patrol office in Westview, that's the next town over."

"Border Patrol? I thought this would be a police matter. Missing persons."

"Leeman says your brother was photographing some rock formations south of here. Rockridge is twenty miles from the Mexican border, Ms. Teel. I don't need to tell you what kind of trouble that causes. This is a dangerous town." She patted her hands on the folder. "*Very* dangerous."

Anita blinked as she left the relative cool of the police station and headed back to the car. Her thoughts spun in dizzying circles. Drew was missing, and the police weren't convinced it was foul play. She had to admit with his erratic behavior at work and skipped rent payments, his character wasn't exactly unimpeachable. He'd managed to keep her away from his apartment and his office during her last visit.

And I didn't do much to further his cause. She mentally kicked herself for her attitude.

Figuring the best course of action was to talk to Leeman and then head to Drew's apartment, she wrenched open the car door, ducking away from the blast of heat. As she bent to slide behind the wheel, her gaze fastened on the deflated tire. Then on the other. She ran around and checked the other side. Four tires, completely flattened, the jagged holes showing where they'd been punctured.

She got out and slammed the car door so hard the windows rattled. Who would vandalize her car right in front of the police station? Her mind flew to the stranger in the truck. But that was ridiculous. She'd only just rolled into town. Was it an enemy she'd made on her last visit to Rockridge?

What was she going to do now? She thought about going back in to report it to the police, but she didn't want to have another encounter with Sergeant Williams. She fished around in her purse for the number of the rental car company and dialed.

We are unavailable at this time. Please leave a message and we will get back to you as soon as possible.

She clicked the phone shut. Drew was out there, possibly dying, and she needed a car. Her breath grew short and a panic started to twist through her stomach. Drew. She had to find him before it was too late.

He was all she had left.

A movement on the sidewalk startled her. She looked up.

The detail that caught her attention first was his eyes, those piercing blue eyes that had lingered in her mind since she'd fled this rugged state. They were the same eyes she remembered, vivid, determined. Angry.

His chin was stubbled, his thatch of short, dark hair tousled. The casual demeanor did not jibe with the expression on his face. His lips were closed in a tight line as he tapped his baseball cap against his muscular thigh.

Her mouth went dry. "Booker."

TWO

Booker shoved his hands into his pockets and forced his voice into as pleasant a tone as he could manage. "Hello, Anita. Did they find Drew?"

She gaped at him. "How did you…?" Her attention was diverted by the big dog that trotted over and inclined his head for a scratch.

"Heard it from a bank teller. Pays to know where the action is in this part of the world." He saw the fatigue and worry on her face vanish behind a mask of self-control. Ace basked in her gentle touch. Clearly the dog didn't have as good a sense of character as he'd thought.

Anita bent down to scratch Ace behind the ears. "Hi, boy. I'm glad to see you. Looks like you're getting around pretty good."

Booker shoved his hands in his pockets as the dog stared at her with devotion in his eyes.

The tenderness in Anita's voice disappeared as she straightened. "They haven't found Drew. I'm not sure they're devoting enough manpower to his case."

"I'm sure you told them so." He didn't bother to hide the sarcasm.

She opened her mouth to answer and stopped, as if she couldn't find any words that would work.

She was never short on words, he thought, and the look of

uncertainty on her face nagged at him. He let the silence linger for a while. "I hope they find him. He's a good guy."

"I didn't know you two were friends."

He allowed himself a slight smile. "He took some pictures in my mine tunnels at your request, remember? I showed him around some spots on my neighbor's ranch, too. We talked for a bit while he was doing the shoot." She remembered all too well; he saw it by the tightening of her mouth, the self-righteous set to her chin. She'd used the pictures as part of her bid to persuade the town council to deny him the right to work the mine on his property. What had Leeman given her in exchange? A feature in his magazine? A nice donation toward her research? It still stung, but what hurt more was the way she'd trampled his heart in the process, as if he had meant no more to her than a stranger. Had he actually told her he loved her? It seemed unreal now. And had she stood there dumbstruck and then turned away without a word? He'd convinced himself they could have something special, but he'd learned the hard way it had all been gut-wrenchingly one-sided. Dumb cowboy, dumb mistake.

Anita cleared her throat. "Well, anyway, I'm going to search until I find him, police or no police. I was headed over to the magazine, but I hit a snag." She gestured to the car. "Someone flattened my tires."

He wondered how she'd managed to make an enemy already. Whoever it was had left him to wrestle with an uncomfortable decision. Should he walk away, let her beg a ride from someone else, abandon her like she'd done to him? Something about the lift of her chin and the tiny tremble in her full lips tugged at his heart. There was a carefully controlled desperation in her that called to something deep inside him.

Deal with it, Booker. You don't have a choice and you know it. He couldn't leave a lady stranded, even if it was the last lady he'd ever want to see again. "I can give you a lift over there, if you want."

Her face pinked, eyes flicking up and down the dusty street as she considered. "Um, well, thank you. It's awfully nice of you to do that for me."

He pulled his keys from the pocket of his faded jeans. "It's not for you. It's for your brother."

She grabbed her purse and followed him to a battered Ford pickup. Ace followed right behind, tail wagging.

Booker stepped ahead of her to wrench open the passenger's door and felt a flush infuse his face as his shoulder brushed hers. "Got hit. Door sticks."

She climbed up onto the cracked leather seat while he fired up the engine. He could smell her enticing fragrance, a faint whiff of vanilla that made his head swim. How did she manage to smell so nice in the desert heat? He concentrated on cranking up the air conditioner. *Drive, Booker. Get the job done and get this lady out of your life.*

As they pulled onto the road, she examined the neat, hay-scented interior and the plastic bin on the floor filled with maps. "Are you planning a trip?"

He didn't divert his gaze from the front window. "Something like that."

They drove the five miles in silence toward the last place on earth Booker wanted to be.

The buildings along the main street were old, wood-sided structures. The tallest was the post office, covered in a cracking layer of off-white paint. A small church advertised a summer camp, and a few children splashed in a wading pool under the shade of a gangly mesquite tree. Booker waved at a man unloading sacks of grain at Pete's Feed and Supply.

The magazine headquarters was one of the more modern buildings in the town, with a neatly kept cluster of yucca shrubs in the front. Booker turned off the engine and shot Anita a look. He'd given her a ride. That was enough for one day, wasn't it? "I'll wait here."

She hesitated. "Oh, would you come in with me? Just for a

minute? I figure the more people who look concerned about my brother's disappearance the better."

With a sigh, he acquiesced. Ace hunkered down in the shade of a scrubby bush to wait for their return.

A blast of cool air greeted them as they checked in with a harried secretary who ushered them into an office that smelled of stale coffee and cigarettes. Booker squirmed in the chair, trying to figure a way out. A tall, lanky man with glasses and a head of curly brown hair came in. He was followed by Leeman, dressed in pleated trousers.

The curly-haired man smiled and shook their hands. "Hello. I'm Paul Gershwin, Drew's editor. I don't think we met last time you were here. I was on assignment in Europe. You know Cyrus Leeman, I understand."

Leeman nodded at them, smiled at Anita and grasped her hand as he slid into a chair. "Lovely to see you again."

Gershwin extended a hand to Booker. "I didn't catch your name."

Anita spoke up. "This is Booker Scott, he's a…friend. Of Drew's. We're both concerned about my brother."

He nodded. "Me, too. Drew's kind of eccentric. It's not unusual for him to take off for a few days, but I'm worried about that phone call you described to me."

Anita leaned forward. "What was he working on?"

Gershwin opened his mouth to answer when Leeman cut him off. "Who knows? Your brother had a tendency to go off on tangents, if you'll excuse me for saying so. He was likely to stumble on topics that interested him more than what we were paying him handsomely to shoot."

She frowned, surprised at the angry tone from a man who she knew to be completely charming and self-possessed. "What are you getting at, Mr. Leeman?"

"I'm just telling you your brother is not good at following rules. He has been problematic since he came here six months ago."

Anita stared at the editor. "Is that what you think, too, Mr. Gershwin?"

Gershwin took off his glasses and polished them on his wrinkled shirt. "He came through when it counted. Never missed a deadline. That's all that matters to an editor."

"Have you heard from him at all?"

Gershwin shook his head. "No. I was hoping you would say you'd talked to him again."

"Only that one quick call, but it was a bad connection so I couldn't understand what he was getting at. Please tell me where you think he was shooting. At least that's a place to start."

The editor handed her a photocopied map and pointed. "Somewhere around here. He was supposed to get us some shots about wind erosion. He said something about photographing a place southwest of here called the Painted Cliffs."

Booker glanced at the map with a frown. "That's no-man's-land. Did he go alone?"

Leeman cleared his throat. "We have no idea. He never bothered to keep us apprised of his actions. We'll certainly let you know if we hear from him. Now if you'll excuse us, we have some layouts to look at."

Anita stood. "Mr. Leeman, you don't seem to have much regard for my brother. It's almost as if you're glad he's gone. When I was here in the spring, you never once mentioned problems with Drew."

"That would have been a betrayal of privacy, I believe, and, anyway, during your last visit we were concerned with saving an endangered colony of bats, as I recall." He shot Booker a look of triumph before he gave Anita an apologetic nod. "To be perfectly honest, Ms. Teel, your brother didn't fit in well here at *Wild World.* As a matter of fact, I intended to let him go after the erosion piece was done."

Booker heard her inhale sharply. He couldn't squash a surge of satisfaction. About time she saw Leeman's dark side.

"And did my brother know that? That you were going to fire him?"

Leeman gave her a polite smile. "I have no idea. I'm sorry, I must get to another meeting. Trust me that we will provide the police with whatever help they require to find your brother."

Booker trailed Anita out to the truck. She looked as if she didn't know whether to scream or cry. Even Ace's enthusiastic lick didn't bring a smile to her face.

She shook her head. "They act like they're happy he's gone."

"Leeman did, anyway."

"He seemed like a different person than the man I worked with before."

"Maybe you were too focused on your crusade to get a clear picture of him."

Anita jerked. "What's that supposed to mean?"

He clamped his jaw together. A fight would only complicate things, distract them from getting the problem solved and her out of his life. He took a deep breath and stared out the window while the engine idled. "Nothing. I think we'd better go check out your brother's apartment right now."

Her eyes widened. "Why? What's wrong?"

He swiveled his gaze to her face. "We need to figure out if Drew really did go to The Painted Cliffs."

"Where is it, anyway? You said it was no-man's-land."

"It's a place the drug runners use to ferry their stuff over the border."

She gasped. "Drug runners?"

"Uh-huh." He pulled out onto the main road. "If he's there, he really is in trouble."

Booker squelched an odd sense of foreboding as they made it to Drew's apartment building on the edge of town. The setting sun was reduced to a few amber-colored rays, which painted the whole complex—a long strip of fifteen units strung together—in an eerie glow. Each unit featured a metal front door and the same striped awning over the dust-covered windows.

Booker followed her into the super's office, the uneasy feeling growing with every minute. The tiny, birdlike woman was reluctant to hand over the key at first. "The guy's a deadbeat. Hasn't paid this month's rent. I ought to hand the matter over to the police."

"If we find Drew, you can collect that rent he owes you," Booker reminded her.

Finally the lady gave in and handed over the key, promising to check in on them after her soap opera was finished. Anita grabbed it and hurried ahead of him to Drew's door.

As it swung open, she gasped and stumbled backward against his chest. He squeezed her protectively for a moment, feeling her tremble as she regained her balance. Catching a glimpse of the apartment over her shoulder, he gently placed her behind him and entered. "Stay here," he commanded.

Keeping as quiet as he could, he did a careful walk through the mess, checking every closet as he did so. He found her in the front room when he returned.

Her cheeks were flushed, eyes bright with fear and unshed tears. "What happened here?"

The small apartment had been completely ransacked. It had only two rooms; one featured a futon and a small worktable, and had an adjoining bathroom. The other was the kitchen. The entire place had been tossed and dumped. All the drawers were opened and upended on the floor. The furniture was overturned, and bits of splintered wood showed where the rickety frames had given out. Even the canisters of sugar and flour in the kitchen were emptied all over the linoleum.

There was no sign of Drew's laptop or camera equipment, Booker noted as he quickly dialed the police and filled them in. An old *Sports Illustrated* cover served as a wall decoration: Michael Jordan smiling down on the room. Even that had been torn away from the wall at one corner. Somebody had been very thorough.

Anita prowled the small space, taking a sweatshirt from its

spot over the back of the wooden chair and pressing it to her face. Tears glinted in her eyes.

Booker stopped dead, feeling his heart squeeze at the stricken look on her face. Part of him wanted to wrap his arms around her, and the other part, the other part wanted to run. He settled for putting a hand gently on her arm. "You all right?"

She dashed the tears from her cheeks and turned away from him. "Yes, yes, of course I am. Are the police on their way?"

He nodded. "They'll be along when they can." He held up a box of granola bars, empty except for one, and a lone water bottle. "I found these in the kitchen. If I had to guess, I'd say he packed up some supplies before he left. There's a can of peanuts on the table, too, sort of like he couldn't fit it into his pack." He hesitated. "Any chance he went out for some recreation, target practice, maybe?"

"No. Drew hates guns. He could never bear to shoot my father's pistol, even." She sank down onto the futon. "What does it mean? Who would want to trash his place? Do you think he ran into trouble from the drug runners?"

"Doesn't help to jump to conclusions. Let's leave here before we disturb any more evidence, and then we'll come up with a plan for tomorrow."

"Tomorrow? I want to go look for him tonight. He might be hurt, or worse."

"No."

"No? Why not? I know you're mad at me, but don't take it out on my brother."

"I'm not doing anything of the kind, Anita. Just listen for once." Booker held up a hand and kept his voice level, meeting those intense brown eyes full-on. "We can't go there at night, not without some prior planning. It's just too dangerous, and Drew wouldn't want you doing a fool thing like that."

She looked down at her tightly clasped hands and he wondered if she was going to listen to reason.

"I guess you're right," she said finally. "I'll rent another car in the morning and go then."

"Never mind that. I'll take you." He was surprised that the words spilled so readily from his mouth.

She blinked. "Why would you do that?"

Yeah, why would you do that, Booker? He gritted his teeth. *Because I'm completely insane,* he wanted to tell her. *Out of my mind to get involved with you again, when the smallest memory of you still makes me crazy.* He understood the anger she kindled inside him, the hurt. What he couldn't wrap his mind around was the strong need that rose in his gut, the need to protect her, in spite of everything.

He cleared his throat and pointed to a small cardboard box next to the television. "Because your brother also packed those."

Anita read the printing on the box aloud.

"Techshot Pistol Cartridges. Low Recoil."

THREE

The nicest hotel in Rockridge happened to be the only one in that small town. Anita tried to ignore the feelings of déjà vu that plagued her as she checked in. The room was clean, painted in soothing shades of green, and the bed was relatively comfortable. Nonetheless, Anita slept only in fits and starts, waking several times fighting off a feeling of terror. The question kept burning at her. What was Drew doing with a gun? Where had he gone, and why hadn't he called her again? Who destroyed his apartment?

The possible answers terrified her even more than her questions. The only island of comfort was Booker, and that scared her, too. She finally dragged herself out of bed after sunup and into a hot shower before calling the rental car company. There was no way she would allow Booker to become her personal taxi service. She'd told him so in no uncertain terms. She couldn't get close to him again. She wouldn't allow herself to.

She sat staring at the phone. While she lingered in a cozy hotel room waiting for the rental car company to get her a replacement, what was happening to her brother? Fear drove her to the window. The sky was an iron gray, layered thick with angry clouds.

The helplessness of her situation swelled inside her until she thought she would burst. She settled for throwing her shoes at the door. They cracked into the metal with a satisfying *thwack*.

A soft knock followed the *thwack*. "Great. Now I've got the neighbors mad at me."

She opened the door to find a startled Booker on the other side. He wore his customary worn jeans and T-shirt with a Windbreaker thrown over it. A Cardinals baseball cap caught the first few drops of rain.

He looked uneasy. "Something hit the door."

She forced a calm tone. "It was nothing. The rental car company is bringing me a car sometime later today. Like I told you before, you don't need to take me anywhere."

He leaned his weight on one hip, crossed arms accentuating his wide chest. "Figured I'd give you my cell number in case anything came up." Without meeting her eyes, he handed her a crumpled piece of paper. His calloused fingers touched her hand, and she felt the strength of hard work and long days.

When he looked away at the clouds that massed on the horizon, she sneaked a glance at his profile. His face was tanned as ever, chin square, hair unruly where it curled out from under his cap, just as she remembered. There was a subtle difference, she noticed; deep shadows under his eyes and an unfamiliar haggard look.

A tender feeling stole over her. *Don't get sappy,* she reminded herself. *You did that before, and it almost distracted you from your duty.*

Booker had needed to realize that mining brought nothing but hardship, especially for the delicate creatures on his ranch. She felt a sliver of guilt that she'd hurt him in the process. With a jolt, she realized she'd been staring.

He cleared his throat. "Not my place, but don't go looking for Drew on your own."

Her eyes narrowed. "I'm not a helpless female."

His smile was bitter. "Oh, I know that all too well."

She forced her chin up. "Thanks for your concern, but it isn't necessary."

He looked at her, eyes searching hers as though he was looking for something he had left.

She tried to think of something, anything, to say, but Booker turned away, mumbled a goodbye and took off in his truck.

She watched him go. A strange thought danced in her mind. If he wasn't so stubborn, would things have turned out differently between them?

No, Anita. You two are incompatible species. You walked away at just the right time, for once, like you should have done with Jack. If only she'd had the strength to walk away from him, maybe her confidence wouldn't be so trampled. She closed the door and headed back to the phone, redialing the number Sergeant Williams had given her for the local Department of Homeland Security, aka the Border Patrol.

Yes, they were still aware of her brother's situation, including the break-in. Someone would call her.

Later.

Though the wall of clouds was intensifying, Anita felt if she didn't move, her body would simply explode. She pulled on the only jacket she brought—a thin, purple nylon affair that could roll up small enough to fit in a pocket—and made sure to take her satellite phone.

The air held a tinge of humidity, the clouds seeming to press on her with a great weight. There was nothing close to the hotel, nothing but a tiny gas station with a mini-mart attached. Sucking in a determined breath, she headed through the buffeting wind.

The whisper-thin man behind the mini-mart counter shot her a curious look. His tufts of white hair gave him a clownish air. "Morning. Help you with something?"

"I'm just here for a few supplies." Scurrying down the nearest aisle, she gathered a handful of sundries: bottled water, trail mix, a couple of apples and a box of Oreos. If she was going to be on the verge of panic for a while, the Oreos would definitely help. She lugged the supplies to the counter and pulled out her wallet.

On impulse, she showed the clerk the picture of Drew. "I'm looking for my brother. Have you seen him?"

He slid on a pair of bifocals and peered at the picture. "No, ma'am. I'm sorry to say I haven't."

Her heart fell. "It was a long shot. Thanks, anyway."

He added a folding umbrella to her pile with a wink. "I think maybe you're gonna need this. On the house."

She thanked him and turned to go when her eyes fell on a stack of leaflets. Booker's smiling face was printed on the top, under the words Living Desert Tours. She shoved one into her pocket and stepped into the swirling wind, her thoughts whirling around just as erratically. Opening the umbrella and avoiding the water that had puddled on the pavement, she jogged back to her hotel room.

Her upper torso was the only part that escaped being drenched. She peeled off the wet clothes, pulled on a robe and spread the paper out on a cracked table, worn and ringed by countless cups of coffee.

Looking to experience the desert in a whole new way? Call Booker Scott at Living Desert Tours. Half-day and full-day trips. Lunch included.

She read the paper twice more. Why was Booker hawking desert tours? He was a cattle rancher with his hand in the opal-mining business. How much time did the man have? And more important, why did thoughts of Booker seem to fill up her mind at every opportunity? She crumpled the paper and threw it in the garbage.

A half hour later, after a lunch of trail mix and cookies, Anita's nerves threatened to burn right through her skin. The police had no updated information on her brother's whereabouts.

"We're pulling in volunteer deputies to help with the search, Ms. Teel. An officer is taking prints and pictures at your brother's apartment. We'll call you if we find anything at all."

She hung up and watched the hands of the clock creep inch by painful inch. The piece of paper Booker had given her materialized in her fingers. "I can't call him." The very idea made her cringe. After their troubled past, how could she ask him for help? She had no right.

The thought of being in the truck with him again sent an odd shiver down her spine. It was not an altogether unpleasant sensation.

She shook the thought away and grabbed the phone. Her brother was counting on her. She could not, would not, let her pride get in the way.

He answered on the second ring, his voice low and husky. "Booker."

"It's Anita. Look, I'm really sorry to bother you but—"

"It's fine."

She took a deep breath. "I need to go to the cliffs, where Drew was headed."

There was a long silence. "I was afraid you were gonna say that."

Twenty minutes later, Booker suppressed a sigh as he jumped out of the truck and wrenched open the passenger side for Anita. Why was he dropping everything to run to her side? Because it was the right thing to do, to help a person in need, he told himself, like he'd done when Mrs. Whitley from church needed her cat dislodged from where it had gotten wedged behind the Sheetrock. So what if it was inconvenient and time-consuming? It was still the right thing to do. He risked a glance at her delicate profile. He'd never had these crazy feelings in his stomach while helping Mrs. Whitley, that was for sure.

Redirecting his thoughts to the foolhardy mission he'd undertaken, he eased the truck onto the main road and headed for the highway. Raindrops pattered the windshield. "Storm coming today. Not a great idea."

"The rain has tapered off from this morning. I'm sure it will be all right. I want to get a sense of the place he was headed, that's all."

He shook his head. "Suit yourself."

She twiddled with her jacket zipper. "How is your father?"

"Not great. He's in one of those retirement villages. Wanted him to stay on the ranch, but he insisted he'd be a bother."

"I'm sorry."

He picked up on a warmth in her voice, remembering how her visits in the spring had cheered his father tremendously. He knew Pops would approve of his helping Anita, in spite of their history. His father would never let a woman down. He'd been there through his wife's illness, unflinchingly devoted, even when her mind was gone and she didn't know who any of them were. Pops was a true gentleman, Booker knew, the kind of man he could only hope to be someday. The resolve crystallized inside him. He would help her, he would find Anita's brother because it was the godly thing to do, and then he would walk away. He tuned back into the present.

"I'll say a prayer for him," Anita said haltingly.

Booker nodded. "'Preciate that."

They lapsed into silence as the miles rolled by, flatland dotted with mesquite and jimsonweed. The sky had lightened to a silver hue, silhouetting the distant mountains in sharp relief. Since the rain eased off, he rolled the window down a fraction to breathe in the scent of newly washed earth.

Rounding a sharp turn, he slowed the truck.

"Why are we stopping?"

"Road dips into a canyon up ahead. With a good rain there's the potential for flash flooding."

"It's not even raining that hard right now."

He glanced at the sky. "It will."

"Booker, we've got to keep going. My brother is out there somewhere."

He ignored the desperation in her voice. "Impatience gets you dead in this place."

"You've got to listen to me. I…" Her words dropped off as the rain began to sheet and then to pound with a fury. It slammed into the truck so hard it bounced off again like tiny glittering bullets. Anita cried out at a crash of thunder.

Booker shot her a brief glance. "Don't worry. It'll stop in a minute or two."

The roar faded to a hum and then a trickle, the storm easing up as fast as it started.

Booker was ready to start the truck when he frowned into the rearview mirror.

An SUV pulled in behind them with Border Patrol emblazoned on the side. A stocky, dark-haired man got out and edged to the driver's side of Booker's truck.

"Mr. Scott, it's Agent Rogelio. You've got Anita Teel with you?"

Booker called out the open window. "Yes, sir."

The agent leaned his head in. "Paul Gershwin told me you might be coming up here looking for your brother."

Booker and Anita got out and followed Rogelio away from the road, to the rust-colored shoulder.

"I got your message," Rogelio continued. "I was going to call you this afternoon."

"Any word on Drew?"

He shook his head. "Not that I've heard. I met your brother a few times, poking around with his camera."

Anita's voice cracked. "Really? When did you see him last?"

"Couple weeks ago. Headed out the same way you are." Rogelio folded his arms across his wide chest. "I've got to be honest with you. I told your brother that he was an idiot."

Booker saw Anita jerk backward a fraction at his angry tone. "That's no way to talk to the man's sister."

"No disrespect intended, but my job's intense. I go around with a target painted on my back. That's my choice. But I don't appreciate having to spend time and energy rescuing thrill seekers who get themselves in too deep, especially when they've been warned repeatedly."

Booker cocked his head. "Drew's doing a job, not sightseeing, and, anyway, what's done is done. The guy's missing, and his sister is worried. Isn't her fault."

Rogelio's tone softened. "I'm just telling you that Border Patrol will assist in any way we can, when we're not busting illegals and ducking gunfire from drug cartels. I'm going to give you the same advice I gave him. Go home." He jerked a thumb at the road ahead. "Leave the searching up to law enforcement so we don't have to bail you out of trouble, too."

Rogelio got back into his SUV, pulled a sharp U-turn and peeled away.

Booker helped Anita back into the truck, feeling a slight tremble in her hand. "Not the nicest cop I ever met."

She blinked. "Why is it everyone seems to think Drew deserves to be in trouble?"

He heard the tremor in her voice. "Not everyone. Like I said before, Drew is a good guy. I'll help you if you want to go look for him. Rogelio's right about one thing, though. It's not safe."

She was silent for a moment, examining her hands twisted together in her lap, knuckles white from the pressure. "Why would you go with me?"

He exhaled, recognizing he had just crossed a line that he couldn't turn back from until the job was done. "Because it's the right thing to do and if it was my brother, I'd sure drive through a war zone to find him."

She gave him a watery smile and they continued down the road.

Booker cleared his throat. "We'll only be able to take a quick look before sundown. We can come back tomorrow. Early."

Her face looked vulnerable, like a little girl's. "Thank you. I feel as though…as though I don't have the right to ask you for anything."

"I offered."

She gave him a puzzled look as the satellite phone in her pocket rang, startling them both.

"It's Sergeant Williams," she whispered, when she checked the screen.

Anita held the phone between them so Booker could hear. "Have you found him?"

There was a pause. "Ms. Teel, I'm afraid I've got some bad news."

FOUR

Anita's body went cold. Booker took the phone from her shaking fingers and spoke quietly to the police officer.

His voice was soft. "It's...not far from here. About three miles, off the highway. I'll take you there."

She couldn't answer. Her mind was locked in a nightmare that she'd experienced before when her parents were killed. The phone call, the strange limbo sprinkled throughout with comments from doctors, bits of information from the police.

Drunk driver.

Both killed on impact.

Death was instantaneous.

Instantaneous. How could something that happened in one insane moment change the life of Anita and her brother so profoundly? And now, she was facing the same horror. Her brother, her only family.

The sensation of moisture on her hand made her realize she was crying. Booker handed her a box of tissue. "Anita..."

His voice trailed off as she raised a hand and shook her head. The sympathy in his deep voice would make her crack open into a million jagged pieces. She had to keep it together now, for Drew. He deserved that much from her.

The heat shimmered off the wet road as they pulled up to the accident site after following a lonely, twisted path that seemed to leave civilization far behind. She recognized the spot. She'd done work in a cave several miles from here, home to a colony of Mexican long-tongued bats. She could almost hear their distinctive high-pitched chitters.

If she hadn't been so terrified, the scenery would have charmed her as it had on her previous visit; a vivid blue sky bisected by ornately furrowed cliffs and dotted with clouds. One corner of her mind noticed a hawk floating in lazy circles above them.

Sergeant Williams alternately took pictures and talked into her radio. There was another officer there whom Anita didn't know, and a fire-rescue vehicle. Somehow she got out of the truck and made her way toward Williams.

"Ms. Teel. I'm very sorry."

"Just tell me. What did you find?"

The officer wiped the sweat from her brow and pointed. "Down there. His motorcycle."

Anita walked several yards away to the edge of a steep canyon. A jagged break in the guardrail framed the view below. The twisted remnants of Drew's motorcycle lay broken and smashed several hundred feet down. She could see the helmeted firefighters milling around, the yellow ropes they'd used to descend bright against the brown cliff side.

"Did you find...?" Her voice broke and she tried again. "Did you find my brother?"

Williams shook her head. "No, ma'am. He may have been thrown from the bike. They're looking for him now."

Her heart swelled. "Then he may be alive." She looked from Booker to Williams and saw the doubt on their faces. "But you don't think so?"

"It would be unlikely, ma'am. That was a violent impact, and as far as we can tell the bike's been there for a while."

Anita felt the hope slide out of her. Her breath grew short, and her head began spinning. Booker took her by the arm and led her to the shade cast by the fire engine. He dried the metal bumper with his jacket sleeve and helped her sit.

"Take it easy. I've got some cold water in the truck." He jogged away to return with an icy bottle.

While she took a few sips, Booker walked closer to the accident site. She watched him studying it, the brim of his baseball cap casting a shadow on his face. He spoke for a moment with the police before he returned to her.

"What is it? What are you thinking?"

He shook his head. "Nothing. Let's hear what the rescue crew has to say."

She was glad when he eased his tall frame down next to her. The feel of him seemed to steady her.

A car pulled up.

Paul Gershwin eased his wiry frame from the seat and hurried over to them. "Oh, man. I heard the call on the radio. Is he…? Have they found him?"

Anita's eyes filled. "Not yet. His bike is down there, at the bottom."

Gershwin gave her arm a squeeze and went to talk with the police. When he returned, his face was a shade paler. "I'm not sure what to say, Ms. Teel."

"Please call me Anita."

He looked at his dusty shoes. "I can't believe that's how it would end for Drew."

"It hasn't ended." The words shot out of her like arrows. "He could be alive. They haven't found any evidence to the contrary."

His eyes widened. "Of course, of course. He's such a character, so quick on his feet. If anyone could survive this, he could. Did they find his gear?"

She shook her head, not daring to look at him closely.

"Then there's hope, right?"

She nodded miserably.

"There's always hope. Look, I've got to get back to the magazine. I'll be there for a couple of hours. Here's my cell phone." He handed her a business card. "Please let me know if there's anything I can do." Paul patted her back and left.

Gershwin thought her brother was dead. So did the police and firefighters and probably Booker. The ruined motorcycle added evidence to support the conclusion.

She could not agree with them.

Drew was alive. She believed it with every fiber in her being. She had to.

An hour later Booker watched as the firefighters cleared the scene. Anita sat in his truck, her chin determinedly high, fingers laced together. The irony made him sigh. She'd only been in Arizona a little more than twenty-four hours, and her life was inextricably twined with his once again. It was like some sort of strange magnetic force that pulled them close until something flipped and they repelled each other.

What flipped was her, he reminded himself. He recalled the tenderness they'd shared, the sweet vulnerability that made him fall for her, hard. He knew she'd loved him; he could see it in every touch, every gesture. Then it was gone. She'd come out all teeth and claws to ruin his chance to save his father's ranch and any shot they'd had at a future. *Remember that, Booker. Help her get through this and put her back on a plane.*

When Agent Rogelio pulled up at the scene, Booker felt his stomach tighten. He waited, watching Rogelio discuss the details with the local cops before his gaze slid over to where Booker stood. He surveyed the scene in a leisurely manner before he spoke, out of earshot of Anita.

"Too bad it turned out this way."

Booker kept his face impassive. "Isn't over until they find the body."

Rogelio pulled his hat down lower to shade his eyes. "You know what kind of place this is. One mistake, one chance, is all you get. The desert takes no prisoners."

Booker could not read the man's eyes behind the shaded glasses. Should he share his suspicions about Drew's accident? A twist of doubt caused him to keep quiet about it.

Aren't you out on a limb enough where Rogelio's concerned? "I'm going to take Anita back to her hotel."

Rogelio stopped him. "We're investigating some things about Drew Teel. Things that aren't looking too good for him. Might want to prepare your gal for some bad news."

"She's not my gal."

Rogelio stared at Anita, a hungry smile creeping across his face. "Good to know I've got a shot, then. I like them feisty."

Booker's jaw tightened. *Don't even try it, man.* He held himself frozen to the spot until Rogelio left.

Shaking off the comment, Booker spoke again to Sergeant Williams, who promised to keep them apprised and assured Anita that a search-and-rescue crew would remain at the sight for the next twelve hours.

"I don't feel right about leaving," Anita announced, as he got in the truck next to her.

"They'll call if there's anything. We're in the way here."

Her lips pressed into a thin line, brown eyes fiery. "No. My brother is down there somewhere and I'm staying right here. I'll go find someplace else to sit if you don't want me in your truck."

Uncertainty shot through him. "It's not that."

She picked up on it right away. "What aren't you telling me?"

He shook his head. "Nothing."

"Not nothing. You don't think they're going to find him alive." Tears began to spill down her face. "How can you believe that? He's all I have. He's the only person in the whole world who…" She kept her face turned to him, the agony written plainly there.

He grabbed her hand to stop the anguished flow of words. "That's not what's on my mind, Anita. I've got a strange feeling, is all, but I don't want to mislead you."

Her mouth opened in a shocked gasp. "What? What do you think? Please tell me." Her voice dropped to a whisper and she squeezed his fingers. "Please."

He picked his words carefully. "Something's wrong. This

road." He pulled his hand away to gesture to the desolate stretch. "It doesn't lead to town or to the Painted Cliffs. There's really no reason for Drew to be here. The spot where the bike went over. It's not a sharp turn, wouldn't have been a problem for an experienced biker to manage."

She nodded. "And?"

"And there's nothing in his saddlebags. No provisions, work stuff, camera, anything. No backpack found at the scene." His eyes scanned the horizon. "Williams says it looks like the gas tank was empty."

"So you think maybe the accident was staged? That Drew isn't dead?" Hope sparkled in her eyes.

"Listen. I'm no cop. Just a gut feeling. I don't want to get your hopes up."

"Too late, they're up," she said, flinging her arms around him and kissing his cheek. "Please help me figure out what happened to my brother. I know I'm the last person in the world you want to be with, but I'm asking, anyway. Please."

The pressure of her body pressed to his made his head swim. *You're in it deep now, Booker.*

Anita let go of Booker and hastily slid to the other side of the seat. Her cheeks burned, but she could not ignore the heady feeling of hope that had sprung up inside her. Drew might be alive. Alive. She pressed her hands together and breathed a silent prayer. *Please, Lord. Please don't take my brother from me.*

She opened her eyes to find Booker watching her. "We need to go to the Painted Cliffs."

Booker arched an eyebrow. "What will that accomplish?"

"I don't know, but my brother was headed there, according to Gershwin. He might have left some kind of a clue to his whereabouts, maybe spoken to someone about his situation."

"There's no one there to speak to. The police should handle the search."

She tried to keep the impatience from her voice. "They're

busy with the crash investigation. Besides, my brother didn't involve the police in whatever problem he was having. He must have had a reason." She looked closely at him. "Do you trust the police around here?"

"Williams is okay."

"How about Rogelio?"

Booker shifted on the worn seat. "He's tight with Cyrus Leeman. I don't trust anyone who buddies up to that snake."

She jerked. "I wasn't anyone's buddy, if that's what you're implying. Leeman came to me on an environmental issue that happened to impact your land. I did my job, and so did he."

"Yeah? So you think he's just a great guy out to save the earth, huh?"

The anger in his eyes made her falter. "We did the right thing."

"Glad you can sleep easy at night."

Sleep easy? She'd not had a peaceful night's rest since she left Rockridge. Thoughts of Booker and the dangerous feelings he'd awakened in her had made that impossible. She'd done the right thing, but the cost had been high. She looked at his profile: strong, proud, lined with fatigue and worry. What had her decision cost him?

She pushed the feelings away and took a deep breath. "I've got to focus on the here and now. I need to figure out what happened to my brother. Will you take me? If not, I'll find someone else."

He gazed at the brilliant blue of the sky. "It'll take an hour to drive out there. Won't have much time. We've got to head back before sunset."

"What happens after sunset?"

He didn't look at her as he pulled onto the road. "Desert comes alive."

FIVE

Anita tried not to dwell on Booker's ominous warning as they headed farther away from civilization. She was a wildlife scientist, after all. Nothing in this desert would send her screaming for help. She busied herself checking her phone for any kind of message from her brother. Who would be after him? His salary was good, she imagined, but knowing her brother he hadn't socked away enough fortune to tempt anyone. At times he didn't even make the rent payments. He must have heard something, seen something. Maybe he photographed something he shouldn't have?

She wished she had someone to discuss her wild theories with, but Booker remained silent. It was just as well. They should avoid anything that would rekindle old feelings. *Remember Jack and what could have happened. Drinking, partying, making stupid choices that would have ruined your life if God hadn't saved you. Don't put yourself there again.*

A massive saguaro cactus thrust prickled branches into the late-afternoon sunlight. In the spring, it had been crowned with showy yellow blossoms, a treasure for the bat species she'd been studying. Now it was bare of blooms, a patch of green against acres of chollas and creosote plants with their fuzzy seed capsules thrust out like fingers. There were no cars here, no tourists crazy enough to venture out into the sizzling nowhere.

Booker pulled off down a narrow path that she never would

have noticed. It led to the mouth of a mesquite-lined wash on one side and a massive cliff rising up on the other. The cliff outline was broken up by piles of roughened rock that had broken away and tumbled down, leaving mountains of rubble dotting the ground.

He handed her a bottle of water and grabbed binoculars for them both. "There." He stabbed a finger at a gap between the cliff and a massive rocky outcropping. "Good view from there. Let's go."

She followed him. The heat immediately soaked her in sweat and heated her face until it felt like it would burst into flame. Grateful that she'd remembered to wear a hat, she struggled to match his long strides.

They climbed the sandy cliff trail until they reached the gap. Binoculars ready, Anita scanned the view below. The Painted Cliffs, striped with shades of gold and pink, had earned their name. The recent rain made bits of mica glitter and shine as she strained to see any signs of human presence there.

Nothing.

The only movement came from a golden eagle that soared down to land on a jagged rock far above them. She sagged, head whirling. What had she expected? That Drew would pop up around some rock pile, a smile on his face? She groaned at her own stupidity. That was exactly what she had hoped.

Booker lowered his binoculars and looked at the sun sinking into a swirl of sherbet colors behind the cliffs. "We've got to go. Gonna get dark fast now."

She nodded. "Okay. I just want to climb to that lower ridge there first. I'll have a view of the whole place."

He frowned. "Bad idea."

"I'll be careful. It will only take a minute." She saw his jaw tighten.

"Really bad idea."

"I'm familiar with the outdoors, Booker," she snapped. "I don't need your permission. As a matter of fact, why don't you head back to the truck and I'll meet you there?" She didn't wait for his answer, instead spinning on her heel and charging down the path that spiraled toward the ridge. Keeping up a brisk pace, she covered a half mile of twisting path before she ventured a look back. Booker was nowhere in sight.

The rock walls rose up around her, muffling the sound of any approaching feet. It was indeed growing darker by the minute, she thought ruefully. Resolutely, she continued on one of two paths that now snaked downward into a shadowed canyon. She made another half mile before the trail widened into a sort of cathedral-like cave, ribboned with veins of color and illuminated only by the faint light that still shone through a crack of rock above her.

It was the kind of scene Drew would wait hours to shoot, until the light was perfect. Fear shook through her again. There was no sign of her brother here, just as there had been none at the crash site. If he was alive, why hadn't he contacted her? Or the police?

The cave grew suddenly dark. Anita knew she had stayed too long. Skin prickled in goose bumps, she realized there was still no sound of Booker's approach. He must have taken her at her word and returned to the truck.

Fine. I can make it back there by myself. She was so intent on picking her way across the floor of the rubble-strewn cavern, she did not hear someone fall in behind her.

A hand, hard and calloused, grabbed her and she was jerked backward off her feet. In a moment she was sitting on a patch of loose gravel, looking into the dark face of a man who held her mouth closed with one hand and kept an arm pressed firmly across her throat, pinning her to the rocky wall.

He slowly moved his arm away from her throat and a knife materialized in his hand. Her blood froze as he held it in front of her eyes. His voice was softly tinged with a Spanish accent. "If you scream, you die."

Fighting to keep the panic from totally overwhelming her

senses, she managed a slight nod. He slowly withdrew the hand from her mouth, knife still hovering close to her face.

He was short, dressed in jeans and a vest that bulged with pockets. A radio clipped to his belt made soft static noises as he stepped back slightly to examine her. "Who are you?"

"My name is Anita Teel." She was surprised her voice worked at all over the fear that seemed to infest every nerve. "Who are you?"

A tiny smile curved his lips and he pushed back the black hair from his face. "It does not seem to me you are in a position to ask questions." He turned the knife so it caught the last remaining light. "Why are you here?"

She forced herself to sit up straight. "Why is that your business?"

He did not smile this time. "Everything that happens in this part of the desert is my business. I ask merely for curiosity's sake. It would be much easier to kill you and be done with it."

She gasped. "I'm looking for my brother. He's a photographer. He was working in the area and he's disappeared." Her phone beeped, but she didn't dare answer.

He ignored the ringing, cocked his head slightly, black eyes studying hers. "I have seen you before, further south. You were here, taking pictures, in the spring. Yes?"

"Yes, I was. But I didn't ever meet you."

"As I said, it's my business to know what goes on here."

The thought of him watching her from a distance all those hours she'd spent without the slightest idea she was under surveillance made her shiver. "Look, I don't care what your business is, and I don't care who you are. I just want to find my brother. Have you seen him?"

"Not…recently."

She leaned forward. "When?"

"He was photographing the cliffs. Perhaps I have seen him since, perhaps not."

The coldness of the rock seeped into her body as she considered. This man might be telling her the truth. Then again, he might be responsible for her brother's disappearance. A distant sound startled them both. The man tensed, listening.

Anita sucked in a breath. It was Booker, and he'd walk unawares into the situation. She opened her mouth to scream to him, when her captor fastened a piece of duct tape over her lips. Frantically, she tried to peel it away but he deftly secured her hands behind her, tying them with a section of nylon rope from one of his many pockets.

He leaned close. "If you will not stay quiet, things will go badly for the person who approaches. And for you."

Eyes round with terror, Anita watched the mouth of the cave, praying that Booker would somehow hear her thoughts.

After Anita's abrupt departure, Booker took a few moments to calm himself down. It wasn't easy. The bullheaded woman was going to get herself killed. Figuring he'd have to sling her over his shoulder and force her back to the truck, he'd headed down the trail until he was stopped by a phone call.

"It's Sergeant Williams. We're going to call off the search for the night. Still nothing to report. Search and Rescue will be back before sunrise to start again."

Booker thanked her and continued on his way to find Anita. After another fifteen minutes, there was still no sign of her. He retraced his steps and took the second trail.

On the way he alternately berated himself for getting involved and worried that she might have slipped and fallen down the steep cliff side. He tried dialing her phone without success. Calling her name again and again, he hurried his pace.

Something about the cavern entrance ahead made his body tense. If she'd taken the lower path he'd have been able to spot her. That left the cavern ahead, but she should have heard his calls by now. Why hadn't she answered him? His pulse quickened.

Lord, please let her be okay. He took a breath and plunged into the dim cavern.

He saw Feria instantly, standing ready with his knife and poised to strike.

Booker froze, his hands away from his body. He frantically shot a glance around the space for Anita and saw her, gagged, staring at him with pleading eyes. "She's no concern to you, Feria."

Feria did not lower the knife. "Maybe no. Maybe yes. She does not belong here."

Booker nodded. "That's what I tried to tell her."

The gleam from Feria's toothy grin shone in the darkness. "She should have listened. You are connected with this lady, then?"

"Just helping her out."

"I see. I do not like intruders."

Booker didn't move. "Neither do I, but that hasn't stopped you from trespassing on my property."

"You will be compensated."

"So you say."

Feria considered. "Most men, I would not let walk out of here. But since we may have business in the future, I will allow you to go."

"And the girl."

He shook his head. "No. She stays."

Booker took a step closer. "She comes with me. She's got no interest in your life, only her brother. She won't make trouble for you. You have my word."

"I am not sure what your word is worth yet, Mr. Scott, but if I find out it's only talk, you will pay the price."

Booker's stomach tensed in an angry knot. His voiced hissed through the cavern before he could think better of it. "If you hurt Anita in any way, you will answer to me."

Their eyes locked until finally, with a slight smile, Feria lowered his knife. "I admire a man with courage." He stepped away from Anita.

Booker went to her, quickly untied the ropes around her wrists and peeled away the duct tape.

As he helped her stand on unsteady legs, Booker noticed that Feria was gone. He gathered Anita in his arms and tried to still the violent trembling that shook her body. "It's okay."

She kept her forehead pressed to his chest and he buried his cheek in the soft down of her hair. Thinking about what could have happened made him squeeze her tighter. If he had been moments later... He didn't allow himself to finish the thought.

She pulled away and took a shuddery breath. "I got the feeling he might know something about my brother. Who is he?"

"I only know him by Feria. He's a drug smuggler, operates caravans of product that come over the border. He routes them through this area to distribution points where the cargo is shipped out."

She gaped. "He's a drug smuggler? How does he know you?"

Booker let her go and led her to the mouth of the cavern. "You don't want to know."

"Yes, I do. He said you have business. What did he mean by that?"

"Nothing. Let's get going." He switched a flashlight on and stepped into the darkness.

She grabbed his shoulder. "It's not nothing. You were talking about some sort of deal with him."

He turned to face her. "Yeah, we talked and now you're safe. If you'd have listened in the first place, none of this would have happened. You can thank me anytime."

She leveled a look at him that made him squirm. "You're not involved with a drug dealer, are you, Booker?"

The frustration overwhelmed him. "That's none of your concern. I'm not mining on my property, so your bats are safe. It's not for you to worry about how I'm managing to make ends meet." He charged off into the darkness, leaving her to follow.

Self-righteous, ungrateful, nosy. He grumbled the words under his breath as they walked.

You're not involved with a drug dealer, are you, Booker?

How had he managed to get in the situation where she would suspect him of it?

If the Lord didn't help him find a way out of this mess soon, he'd be the one lost in no-man's-land.

SIX

Anita stayed silent on the drive back to her hotel. Her head was filled with dark images. Her brother lost, Feria standing over her, and fear that Booker was somehow involved with him. Booker's admonishment was right, of course. His business didn't concern her, but the fact that he might have gotten caught up with a drug dealer made her insides tremble. Was he that desperate? She decided to find out more about Booker's ranch if she could.

His jaw was still set in a stubborn line as he dropped her off and told her what time Search and Rescue would return to the accident site.

"Got a job to do tomorrow, but I'll get you a loaner car," he said as he wrenched open the door and helped her from the truck. "Easier than relying on that rental company."

"I'll be okay."

He looked at her, his face softening. "Look, I'm sorry about yelling at you. And I'm glad that everything turned out all right with Feria."

She gazed into his eyes, lit by the moon, and saw grief and worry there that she hadn't noticed before. *Had* everything turned out all right with Feria? She wasn't so sure.

True to his word, she found a note from Booker slid under her door the next morning.

Chevy belongs to a friend. Radio's busted but she drives okay. B

She smiled as she climbed in the old truck and headed to the crash site, breathing prayers as she drove. Her nerves grew more agitated with each passing mile. Had they found him? Had her brother crawled away from the crash site and gotten shelter in some rocky crevice? Or had he been too badly injured to survive in the desert? She swallowed hard, thinking about her own near deadly nocturnal encounter.

Sergeant Williams sipped from a cup of coffee. The temperature was already climbing as the sun unfolded around them.

"No sign of him yet, Ms. Teel."

Anita took a steadying breath. "Sergeant, do you know a man named Feria?"

William's eyes narrowed. "Bad dude. Why?"

Anita told her about their confrontation, leaving out the part about Booker's strange mention of a business deal.

Her eyebrows lifted. "You do tend to attract trouble, Ms. Teel. Tires slashed, brother gone and Feria." She whistled. "I'll alert Border Patrol. They'll be interested to know his whereabouts." She retrieved a clipboard from the car and wrote down Anita's statement.

As they were finishing up, a sweaty firefighter in brush gear made his way over to them.

Anita shot to her feet. "Did you find him?"

He shook his head. "No, ma'am. We've got to pull out of here."

She blinked. "Pull out? What do you mean? You can't leave with my brother out there, alone."

He sighed. "We're very sorry, ma'am, but we're needed elsewhere."

Williams spoke up. "We'll continue to look for your brother as much as we can. We've got bulletins out to all other local agencies so we can follow up on any leads."

Anita's heart felt as though it shriveled up. She watched in a daze as the firefighters packed up their gear and drove away.

A tow truck secured Drew's motorcycle under Williams's supervision before she turned to Anita.

"Do you want me to drop you somewhere?"

Anita shook her head. "No." She waved a hand absently to the truck. "I've got a loaner."

"Are you okay to drive?"

The officer's voice held a touch of kindness that made Anita feel like crying. Instead she forced herself to straighten. "I'm fine. I will look into some things on my own until my brother is found."

Williams nodded. "Be careful."

Anita suppressed a shiver as she drove away, thinking of Feria. He said he had nothing to do with Drew's disappearance, but he seemed to have eyes and ears all over the vast area. What if he was lying?

Her thoughts returned to the strange conversation he'd had with Booker. There was some connection between the two, in spite of Booker's protests. She drove without realizing her destination until she eased onto the long graveled driveway of Scott Ranch. She looked for Booker's truck. No sign of him.

The last time she'd visited, she'd had to stop a few times to allow passage of the rust-colored Red Brangus cows—or the white Charolias, which stood out so clearly against the green scrub. Now she didn't catch sight of a single one as she drove along. In the distance she could just make out the slowly whirling blades of the metal windmill that pulled water to various tanks.

Like to go to solar panels someday, when we get the money, she remembered Booker saying, recalling the pride that lit his face when he'd told her about his ranch. The thought pained her. She'd loved that boyish quality until she realized it was reminiscent of Jack and the disastrous choices she'd made when love took over. Looking back, she could blame that mess on the desperate need for love and acceptance after her parents' traumatic death, the stress of college life, her own insecurity. Whatever the reason, falling in love with Jack in graduate school left her determined never to repeat the error.

Why am I here? she thought, as she continued up the dusty drive toward the white stucco house. *He wants me out of his life, and I should be busy looking for my brother.* The hard fact was, she had no idea where to turn next, and Booker was the only person in the town she could call…what? A friend? An ally? A confidant? None of the words seemed to fit.

Just deal with it, Anita. She got out of the truck and marched through the blazing sunshine to the front door of the one-story house, which was covered with a tile roof that seemed to shimmer in the light. She was grateful for the shade of a massive cottonwood as she knocked on the door. For a crazy moment, she desperately wanted to be sucked back in time to the spring, when Pops, Booker's father, was there to greet her, his soft voice so like her own father's. She closed her eyes and remembered the moment, sitting in the cool of the house, sipping tea and listening to Pops speak with pride about his son, welcoming her onto their land, into their lives.

Had she betrayed them both? Her thoughts darted off in so many different directions she wasn't sure of anything. When there was no answer to her knock, she got back into the truck and drove slowly, taking in the harsh terrain that miraculously supported a ranch. She found herself driving away from the house, down a graveled secondary trail that she knew well.

The descent into the canyon seemed to transport her back to the moment when Booker first brought her to Mesquite Cave, the entrance to his opal mine. Something drew her here, to him, as it had last spring when she'd first seen it.

The opening was dark against the sunlit brilliance of the canyon wall. She pulled her hat on and moved nearer, but not close enough to frighten the roosting bats. The air, cooled deep inside the earth, funneled out through the cave, bathing her face.

It seemed somehow poetic that the precious colony of lesser long-nosed bats nestled in darkness alongside the sparkling blue precious opals. Treasures, quiet and still, keeping their own secrets until they were disturbed.

Without warning, a shadow fell across her from behind and a hand clapped over her mouth.

Booker gently moved Anita away from the cave entrance and let her go. "Didn't want you to scream and scare your bats."

She was still startled, breathing heavily.

He would have been stopped by how lovely she looked, if he wasn't so angry. "What are you doing here?"

"I wanted to talk to you. You weren't home. I figured I'd do a quick observation while I was here."

"To make sure I haven't been doing a little mining?" He tasted again the bitterness at being told what to do on his own land. His land, his opals that would help pay the bills on this ramshackle place he called home. Moreover, seeing her there brought his stupidity back to him. He pictured the perfect cabochon he'd had polished and set into a pendant for her. It sparkled with a fire inside, the same fire he'd felt for Anita.

He'd never given it to her. Never had the chance after she'd turned on him like a cornered cat. He still didn't understand it. Probably never would. He walked over to his horse and fiddled with the stirrup to keep from saying something he shouldn't.

She stood with her arms folded, staring at him. "Well, have you?"

He bit down on his fury. "No, I haven't set foot in there, so you can take your report back to Leeman and the town council and tell them I've been behaving. Was there anything else you needed to check on?" The horse shifted his weight, reacting to the angry tone. Booker gave the animal a pat on the rump to soothe him.

Her look faltered, became contrite. "Booker, I know you won't believe this, but I wasn't checking up on you. I felt restless. I wanted to see a familiar place, I guess." She exhaled. "I apologize."

The humility took him by surprise. An apology? Maybe this thing with her brother really had given her a different perspective. *Don't bet on it, Booker.* "Any word on Drew?"

"No. They've called off the search. I don't know what to do."

He knew how hard it was for her to admit being helpless. Her cheeks were flushed with heat, and she looked so small, standing there in the shadow of the massive rock face. The last of his anger drained away. "Let's go back to the house. We'll talk it over, figure something out."

She climbed up into her loaner truck and he mounted the quarter horse. They had just started moving when Booker saw a car pull onto the property, heading for the house. Visitors were few and far between on Scott Ranch. He wondered if they'd found Drew's body.

Looking at Anita staring through the windshield, stark fear written across her face, he knew she was wondering the very same thing.

SEVEN

Paul Gershwin met them in the driveway. "Sorry to intrude. I needed to talk to you."

Booker nodded and dismounted, leaving the horse to graze on clumps of dried grass. He led the way into the cool interior of the house. "Come inside."

Gershwin and Anita followed him into the wood-paneled living room.

Booker excused himself and tarried in the kitchen, still trying to decide how to handle things. Part of him resented Anita's intrusion on his property, but the other part, deep in his soul, took flight when he saw her standing there as she had in the spring. Seeing her there, he could almost remember the joy he'd felt when he finally admitted to himself that he loved her. The memory of that disastrous realization unsettled him. Suddenly he pictured his father, who would berate him for leaving both guests sitting there in such an inhospitable manner.

Nothing's changed. Just help her, that's all. Help her and be done with it. He grabbed a pitcher from the refrigerator and filled glasses with tea.

Returning to the living room, he found Anita slightly more composed. "Paul went in the other room to answer a cell phone call."

He nodded, handing her the tea.

"I'm sorry," she said. "For coming here. It's intruding, I know. I'm not sure exactly why I came. I guess I just needed some advice."

He allowed a slight smile. "Pops always says advice is worth what you pay for it."

She smiled back, cheeks flushed from the heat. "I miss seeing your father here."

He nodded, shoving down a wave of pain. "It feels empty without him."

"Where are the cattle? I didn't see any as I drove up."

Booker got up and straightened a pile of papers on the scarred wooden desk. "Sold most of 'em. Only about a hundred heads left."

He heard her gasp. "You sold them? Why?"

"This is dry ranching and we've been in five years of drought. Not enough water, not enough money." *Not enough of anything.*

She paled. "So that's why you wanted to mine the opals on your property?"

He would have told her that before, if she'd only taken the time to listen. "Doesn't matter. That's done. Let's focus on your brother."

She was silent for a moment. "If I could figure out what he'd gotten himself into it might point me in a direction to look."

"Can you call his credit card company? Check out recent activity?"

She shook her head. "No. They won't give me any information. The police are supposedly handling it."

"But you don't think they'll take care of it? You don't trust them?"

"I'm not sure. Williams has been on the ball, but I don't know about Rogelio. What do you think of him?"

It was the question he'd staked his whole future on. Was Rogelio a straight arrow? He'd prayed with all his heart and soul that he'd made the right call about the guy. She sat waiting for his reply. "As I told you before, I think I'd trust him more if he wasn't so chummy with Leeman."

She sighed. "Do you hate Leeman because he sided against you on the mining issue?"

"I don't hate him."

"He's a businessman and an environmentalist. He lives a respectable life. His wife, Heidi, is lovely, too. They even hosted a wonderful dinner for me when I was here last. I'm sorry, but I don't share your opinion of him, even though he doesn't seem to have much respect for my brother."

"You're seeing what he wants you to see."

Anita straightened, eyes blazing. "I'm nobody's patsy."

In spite of his effort, the resentment rose inside him and brought him to his feet. He tried to keep his voice low. "I'm sure Leeman is a swell guy. No particular reason he wanted you to go to the council and persuade them to make my mine off-limits. Just doing his civic duty. Not like he wants to force me off my land, off my father's ranch. Why would an upstanding businessman want to do that?" His words grew louder than he'd intended, echoing off the pine slatted floor.

She blinked. "What are you talking about? Why would Leeman want you off this land? You told me it's parched here, too dry to run your cattle. What value is in it for him?"

"Think about it, Anita."

She opened her mouth to respond, when Gershwin emerged from the hallway.

"Sorry to interrupt," he said, pocketing his phone. "Trying to get the next issue out without Drew is killing me."

Booker gestured for him to sit. "Nothing to interrupt. What brings you here?"

"I need to warn you." He stood uncertainly, arms folded across his narrow chest. "I've always considered Drew a friend and he's never given me any cause to doubt him. I felt I owed it to him and to you to explain things before you run into him."

Booker watched the editor's brow furrow. "Who?"

"Mr. Leeman. He's beyond furious at your brother. He's a passionate man, temperamental, and we've battled plenty, but I've never seen him this angry."

She stood. "At my brother? What are you talking about?"

"It's about Mr. Leeman's wife. You've met her, she's a sweet woman."

"Heidi? Yes, I've met her. She does the books for *Wild World*. What's this got to do with her?"

"Your brother admires her very much. They've been friends since he came to work here. Heidi even helped him with some local contacts when he was starting out at *Wild World*."

She shook her head. "So they're friends. So what?"

Gershwin looked away from Anita, focusing for a moment on his shoes. "They might have been more than friends. It turns out that Heidi bought two plane tickets to Mexico last week."

A bad feeling crept into Booker's gut. "Two?"

Gershwin nodded. "Uh-huh. The second ticket was purchased for a D. Teel."

The bad feeling settled in a hard ball. Booker let out a breath. "Oh, boy."

Anita's mouth fell open. "What? My brother would never have an affair with a married woman. That isn't possible."

"Leeman seems to think it is." Gershwin sighed. "He's on his way to tell the police that Drew seduced her and intended to escort her out of the country. What's more, he's going over the books, looking to see if Drew skimmed money from the company."

Her eyes flashed. "That's ridiculous and a complete fabrication. Is that what Heidi says? Surely she can straighten it out."

"Heidi took off four days ago. She said she was visiting her sister but that was a lie. Turns out…" He hesitated.

Booker stared at Gershwin. "Tell us."

"Turns out she's disappeared, too."

Booker watched as Anita's face turned deathly pale. He stepped closer as she sank into the chair. "Mr. Gershwin, do you have any reason to believe Drew and Heidi were having an affair?"

The man's gaze darted around the room, finally fixing on the view from the front window. "They were friends, kindred spirits, I think. Both very creative, intelligent, easily bored. Heidi was restless, searching for a better life."

"You haven't answered my question."

"They were friends, that's all I can say for sure. Leeman noticed them working together a few times and put the kibosh on it. As far as I know, that's all there was."

Booker eyed Gershwin's faltering glance. *But he doesn't really believe it. He knows something he's not telling.*

Anita cleared her throat. "It doesn't make sense. If they were…together, why would we have found Drew's motorcycle and no sign of her? What about his apartment? The person who slashed my tires? There's more going on here than Drew's friendship with Heidi Leeman."

Booker was glad to hear the fire in her voice. "She's right. It isn't as simple as all that."

"I'm just telling you to be careful. Leeman is a dangerous man. You asked me before what Drew was working on." Gershwin pulled out his keys and an envelope from his pocket. "Here are some pictures from his last shoot. I thought maybe they would help somehow. I didn't see anything significant, but maybe you will."

Anita grabbed the envelope and gave Gershwin a hug. "Thank you."

Gershwin smiled. "Us little guys gotta stand up to the big man. My father worked for a tyrant for twenty years and the guy let him go a week before his retirement. He never recovered. Ended up killing himself. I guess I kind of admire Drew for not being afraid to make a life with Heidi. She deserved better than Leeman."

Booker shook his head. "I still think there's more here than meets the eye."

"Could be. I'm just telling you what I know. Anyway, I've got to get going. Wish I could help more." Gershwin left.

Anita and Booker fanned out six pages of color photographs on the coffee table. They all had a common subject. Anita pointed to the first shot. "What kind of tortoise it that?"

"We call it the desert tortoise, but I bet you science types have a fancier name."

She laughed, a musical sound. "We can go with desert tortoise." She rifled through the pages. "Some great shots here. He must have been doing a feature on them, but I don't see how it will help us find him."

"Maybe it won't, but it might narrow the field." Booker fished a magnifying glass out of the drawer and looked more closely.

Anita sat back, eyes shifting in thought. "I'm trying to recall what, if anything, I know about tortoises. They can live a long time without water."

"Up to a year. Get most of their moisture from the grasses they chow down on in the spring."

"And I think Drew told me they are active when the rain-storms come."

"Yeah, they dig basins to capture the water. That's why they need diggable soil." An idea sizzled to life in his head. He grabbed several pages of the photos and held them to the light by the window. "It can't be. It's too coincidental."

Anita came behind him, her cheek pressed against him to see the photo.

He tried to ignore the tingles in his arm at the pressure. He squinted once more at the photos and turned to face her. "I know where Drew took these pictures."

Anita tried not to let hope carry her away this time. The only thing she'd accomplished at the Painted Cliffs was almost getting herself killed. The chances that the pictures would bring them closer to her brother were minimal. Things were getting worse for him with Leeman's accusations and Heidi's disap-pearance, and she was willing to follow any crazy lead.

"So who owns the property we're going to?"

"Robin Hernando."

Anita thought she heard a tinge of emotion when he said the name. "Is she a friend of yours?"

He nodded. "Yes. Not as close as we once were."

The sunglasses he wore made it impossible for her to read his face. *How close were you?* she wanted to ask. She chided herself for being nosy and ridiculous. Robin was probably a salt-of-the-earth-grandmother type who sat on the porch stringing beans in the evenings.

They drove twenty miles or so down a gradual slope into a valley speckled with cottonwood trees. The land was greener here, patches of grass adorned with tall spiky bushes Anita did not recognize. Several men on horseback passed by, faces shaded by cowboy hats. They waved at Booker and tipped their hats at her.

She noted the solar panel jutting out incongruously against the wild landscape.

"Robin has a nice place," Anita said, as the modern-villa-style house came into view. "How come it's so much greener here?"

"Robin's property sits in the valley. It's a natural draining point from the mountains. She knows how to manage a ranch, too."

Anita heard the admiration in his voice and wondered why it awakened an odd feeling in her. As they passed by a jagged outcropping of rock, a dark face peeked out, shadowed by a battered straw hat. He had a wary look, different from the workers she'd seen.

"Who is that?"

Booker shot a look in the direction she pointed and nodded to the figure before the man disappeared into the shadows. "Name's Diego. Wanders around these parts looking for work and food."

"Has he worked at your place?"

Booker shook his head. "He doesn't have papers, but I've given him some food and let him stay in the shed a few times when the temps dropped into the negative numbers."

"So you're a softy underneath, aren't you?"

He flushed. "Don't let it get around."

They parked, and Robin greeted them at the door.

She was nowhere near grandma age. Anita guessed the statuesque woman to be in her early thirties. Her long hair flowed freely around delicate features. Her full lips curved into a smile at the sight of Booker.

"I'm surprised to see you," she said, throwing her arms around him and kissing him on both cheeks.

Anita felt as though she'd become invisible until Booker disentangled himself and introduced her. Robin clasped Anita's hand, her brown eyes curious under a fringe of thick eyelashes.

"Come in, please." She led them to a richly appointed sitting room, done in a palette of chocolate-browns and deep maroon. Settling herself on a leather couch, she asked the lady who appeared to bring refreshments.

"Are you enjoying your stay here, Ms. Teel? Such a warm time of year to visit."

Anita tried a friendly smile. "I'm not visiting. I'm looking for my brother."

"Oh?" Robin took the iced glass the woman handed her. "Who is your brother? What happened to him?"

Booker declined the iced tea. "His name is Drew Teel. Do you know him?"

Robin blinked, sipping delicately. "The name doesn't sound familiar. Should I?"

"He's a photographer. We think he took some pictures of the tortoises on your ranch."

She cocked her head. "Tortoises. I do remember someone coming to take some shots here, yes, but I'm afraid I didn't really get to know him. My ranch manager takes care of all that."

Booker nodded. "Carlos?"

"Yes. If I may ask, what do you think happened to your brother?"

Anita sighed. "I'm not sure. We're just trying to follow any kind of leads we can to figure that out."

Robin's gaze traveled from her to Booker. "You are lucky, Ms. Teel, to have such a man to help you."

Booker looked slightly uncomfortable. Anita felt a flush creep into her face. "Yes. Booker has been a great help."

Robin continued to look at him intensely until he shifted and cleared his throat. "Have you heard from Heidi?"

Robin stiffened. "Heidi?"

"Heidi Leeman. Last year when I was here, you were talking with her, planning a party, I think."

Robin frowned. "Oh, yes. What a memory you have, darling. How is Heidi?"

"I'm not sure. I thought you could tell me."

"I haven't seen her for months. I meant to call her but I just haven't had a spare minute. Why?"

He shrugged. "Heard a rumor that she was missing. Nothing confirmed. Wondered if you'd heard from her."

"No, I'm afraid not. You know, Booker, it's fortuitous that you stopped by. I was going to give you a call. I need your advice on where to add the next solar panel."

"Why not ask Carlos?"

She eyed him playfully. "Because he's surly, and I'd much rather talk to you."

The vague hostility Anita experienced intensified. Robin wanted more than just advice from Booker, she was sure. Ashamed of her reaction, Anita looked for an escape. "May I use the restroom, Ms. Hernando?"

"It's Robin. There's a guest bath down the hall to your right."

Anita forced herself to walk calmly, though her feet felt like running. What was wrong with her? She had no claim to Booker. Why shouldn't he carry on a relationship with Robin? They were neighbors and colleagues. *And close friends,* she thought ruefully, as she closed the bathroom door on the sound of Robin's laughter.

She ran the tap in the marble sink and let the cool water run over her hands. Then she patted her heated face. Reaching for a towel, she knocked over an elegant covered basket on the counter. The contents spilled onto the floor: a hairbrush, a tube of lipstick and a small compact.

Anita scurried to pile the things back in the basket. As she picked up the hairbrush, something startled her. The bristles were tangled with a few strands of hair, very long and very blond.

It was the exact same shade as Heidi's hair was the last time she'd seen her.

EIGHT

Booker moved away from Robin when Anita returned. "Robin said to go ahead and poke around. I've got a pretty good idea what area of the property Drew was shooting. You game for a little drive? We've got a couple more hours before we start to lose the light."

"Of course." Anita headed toward the door.

Booker hugged Robin. "We'll let you know if we find anything."

She smiled, teeth dazzling white against her dusky skin. "I'll send Carlos out there to give you a hand. I'd come myself but I've got a phone conference with Paul Gershwin. He's trying to finish Drew's story, I believe." She shot a nervous glance at Anita. "I'm sorry. I don't mean to be insensitive. Why don't I talk to him and see if I can find out where Heidi's gone?"

"He told us he didn't know, but thanks, anyway."

"Anything to help."

They climbed into the sweltering truck after he checked to be sure the cooler was stocked with water.

Anita was strangely quiet.

"You okay?"

She turned to him. "What do you know about Robin Hernando?"

Her intensity startled him. "Know? She's from a rich family.

This ranching thing is only a diversion for her. She'd much rather be in Europe or at their villa in Mexico, but her father insists she learn the business."

"How long have you known her?"

"Four or five years."

"Did you two date?"

Booker shifted in his seat. "This is beginning to feel like an interrogation. Why do you want to know?"

"Because she's lying."

He eased the truck toward a graveled trail. "Lying about what?"

"I knocked over a basket in the bathroom and a woman's hairbrush fell out. The hair in that brush was long and blond, just like Heidi's."

"Nice detective work, but it could have been from someone else. Robin has friends stay over frequently."

"I have a feeling it's Heidi's. You didn't answer my question about whether or not you two dated."

He bristled. "Because, as I mentioned, it's not relevant."

"It might be if she's lying and your feelings for her prevent you from seeing the truth."

The exasperation inside him threatened to explode. "Anita, we're here to retrace your brother's steps, not Heidi's. Let's focus on that." He clamped his mouth shut and eased the truck over a nasty pothole.

The waning afternoon sunlight seemed to pour down on them with renewed energy.

Anita stayed quiet as he wrestled the truck along. Just as well, he thought.

They drove across the sprawling property, stopping to let a half-dozen head of cattle cross. Booker tried to suppress the envy. He didn't have enough cattle left to bring in much at auction. The desert tour business was slow, hardly sufficient to help with the feed costs. *Never mind that now. The Lord will provide if He wants you to stay here.*

The thought of leaving the ranch his father and grandfather

had made out of their own sweat and muscle made his stomach clench. Anita pulled him back to the present.

"How do you manage cattle when they are free to wander all over the place?"

Grateful that she wasn't prying about Robin anymore, he relaxed slightly. "Ranchers here don't manage the animals, they manage the water." He pointed to a steel tank, brilliant in the bright sun. "Water tank to supply the ponds. Where the water is, you'll find the cattle sooner or later. Just gotta keep all the windmills working to move the water around, unless you've got solar panels, of course."

"That sounds like a hard job."

He smiled. "It is, but I wouldn't trade it for anything. Give me a good horse and a head of cattle to manage and I'm a happy man." *Mostly happy, anyway.*

They parked at a rocky overlook and a small truck pulled in behind them.

Carlos approached, face expressionless behind his wide mustache. He nodded to Booker, who introduced Anita.

"I understand my brother worked here in the spring, photographing the tortoises."

Carlos nodded. He pointed to the wash below. "Took his pictures down there."

"Did you ever speak to him?"

Carlos shook his head.

He doesn't much speak to anyone, Booker wanted to tell her. "Okay if we take a look?"

He shrugged and turned to go. Anita stopped him.

"Wait, please. I had one more question. Has Ms. Hernando had a houseguest recently? A woman with long, blond hair?"

Booker watched Carlos's eyes narrow.

"Don't think so. Not my business who stays over." He spit on the ground and returned to his truck.

"He could be covering for her," Anita said, watching the truck pull away.

"Or he could be telling you the truth, just like Robin." Booker grabbed a pack, stuffed some water bottles in it and started down the dusty slope. He knew from the sound of the gravel crunching underfoot that she'd fallen in behind him. He cast a glance at the sky and hurried his pace.

By the time they reached the bottom, they were both coated with sweat and panting from exertion. He headed toward a rock overhang and handed Anita some water. Training the binoculars over the irregular ground, he found what he was looking for. "Just over there, the earth is softer, good for digging burrows. I saw some tortoises when I was here last year."

He thought she was going to comment, but instead she pulled her hat down farther on her forehead. The look of sheer determination on her small face made him want to pull her close. It was that passion that captivated him, because he'd felt the same level of passion for his land, for his family. He wished he could throw away what had happened and start again. His gut told him it was impossible, but the thought tantalized him nonetheless.

She marched by him, crunching over the ground at a quick pace. "Come on. We're wasting time."

Not bothering to hide his smile, he headed after her.

Anita mulled it over as she hiked. If Robin was a friend of Heidi's, perhaps she knew where the woman went. Like it or not, Drew's whereabouts were somehow linked to Heidi's, she was sure. So what reason would Robin have for covering up the truth? She would find out, whether Booker liked it or not.

They came to the bottom, a rocky plateau studded with irregular projections of rock and a clump of twisted cottonwood trees. Booker took out the pictures Gershwin had given them.

"There." Anita pointed to the picture. "That L-shaped rock formation." She scanned the horizon. "It's that one, isn't it? Drew was taking pictures from over there."

She didn't wait for his answer. Her body found a new source

of adrenaline as she hurried to the spot. It was not visible from higher ground. A bowl-like depression tucked behind the boulders made the perfect spot for tortoises' burrows.

Booker arrived behind her. He spent a moment looking closely at the ground. "Here. You can see where the tortoises have dug their basins to catch the summer storm water. They're probably underground right now, but as dusk approaches they'll come out to feed."

In spite of her anxiety about her brother, Anita couldn't help but marvel. "So amazing, the way they pull what they need from this place." *God gives them bounty in the midst of hardship.* She cast a look at Booker. Would God give him bounty enough to hold on to his ranch? She hadn't made it easier, she knew. Stifling a wave of guilt, she picked her way across the rusty earth, now painted in rich color by the waning sun.

Booker followed behind. "Gotta head out soon. Sun's going down."

"Right." She scanned the ground, feeling her heart sink with every passing moment. *Drew, where are you? What happened?*

Booker suddenly shot out a hand. "Look."

She followed his gesture. Hidden almost completely in the earth was a small wooden structure, no more that eighteen inches across. It rose only about ten inches off the ground. Covered as it was by earth and scraggly weeds, she would have missed it entirely.

"What is it?"

They moved closer. "A blind, I think."

She gasped. "Just enough room for the photographer to lie down in while getting his pictures."

Booker nodded and gave her an uneasy look.

She made a move to run to the blind but he stopped her.

"Let me check it out first."

She looked into his face and saw gentleness and concern there. He was worried what they'd find in that dark place, and it touched and scared her at the same time. Unable to speak, she nodded.

He crept closer until he knelt next to the blind and leaned down to look into the opening. Then he straightened and called her over.

Anita's nerves propelled her in a run to the spot. "What is it?"

He reached into the space and pulled out a small case. "Camera. Is it Drew's?"

Hardly able to breathe, she took it in her hands and read the small ID tag: D. Teel. Eyes filling, she nodded. "Yes. It was his backup camera."

He reached an arm around her shoulders. "Okay. We're getting closer, then."

She opened the top of the case. Something shot out across her arm. She screamed and dropped the camera, scrambling backward until she tripped over a rock and landed on the warm ground. "What was that?"

The flash of golden fur vanished behind the nearest rock.

Booker looked as though he was trying to hold in a chuckle. "Kangaroo rat. Sorry. Didn't know there was a hitchhiker."

Anita felt a smile growing on her own face. She couldn't help but think Drew would have gotten a huge laugh out of the whole thing. She took Booker's hand and he hauled her to her feet. She started to open the camera case, gingerly this time. Hoping the batteries hadn't died, she turned on the power button.

The camera gave a comforting beep. She switched the functions until a series of thumbnail pictures filled the screen. Feverishly she sped through them. Many were tortoise shots, cliff-side pictures and several close-ups of coyotes. Thinking about how he'd gotten those shots made her shiver. At the end, the last three frames were different. She thought they were blank, at first, or the camera had malfunctioned, until she hit the full view.

They both leaned forward to peer closely.

"It's pictures of some sort of text. Columns and rows of…?" She struggled to see.

Booker took a turn staring at it. "Numbers, maybe. Can't tell for sure. We're gonna have to download it to the computer."

She looked at him in surprise. "I didn't know you were tech savvy."

"Thought I was just a dumb cowboy, huh? I can do the basic computer stuff, but that's about it."

She laughed. "You're a man of many surprises."

"That's me. Let's go get this back to my place and see what we can figure out."

For the first time, Anita felt like they were getting closer to finding her brother. As they struggled back up the trail to the truck, the sun disappeared on the horizon. The stars began to glimmer in a sky that seemed to have no end.

Booker opened the truck door for her, but she paused to look up at the cathedral above them. "It's so beautiful."

"Yes, it sure is."

She realized he was not looking at the sky when he said it. A mixture of pleasure and fear filled her up. With a start, it dawned on her that the emotions she felt so strongly for Booker in the spring were still there.

Her mind flashed back to a dorm room, filled with people and smelling of beer and nachos.

"Come on, Anita." Jack's face was perfect, handsome, chiseled. *"Have a drink. You need to loosen up."*

She declined.

"Look around, honey. People are having fun, everyone but you."

She saw the frown of disapproval on his face.

"You don't have to be so uptight all the time. College is supposed to be fun, too. Here, just one." He handed her a bottle and watched while she took a few sips. *"There's a girl. Now, don't you feel better?"*

Though she was pleased to see him smile, happy to be pulled into the circle of his arms, she still felt oddly out of place in the room full of celebrants. He'd brought her another drink later. She didn't want any more, but she desperately wanted Jack to be happy with her. It pained her how easily she'd given up who she was in the pursuit of love.

The throb of the engine brought her back to the present. She put thoughts of the past away and clutched the camera close, as if it still held some warmth from her brother's hands. He was her priority now. *Please, God. Help me figure out what's happening to my brother.*

It was completely dark now, no streetlights to pave the way. In the distance, she could make out the cheerful lights of Robin's house.

The truck bounced and jostled as they headed down the winding slope.

The day was catching up to Anita and she found her eyes getting heavy.

She saw Booker tense before she heard the sound.

Jerking upright she was blinded by the glare of headlights. It took a moment for her brain to put it together. She screamed as the car bore down on them.

NINE

Booker wrenched the steering wheel and managed to avoid a head-on collision. The truck slammed across the uneven ground until he wrestled it back on the trail.

Whoever it was spun the car in a shower of flying gravel and pulled in behind them again. Booker gunned the gas as hard as he dared. Rocks hemmed them in on one side of the trail. On the other side was a drop-off to a dry riverbed.

The truck shot ahead along the dark road.

Anita's voice called above the noise. "Who is it? Are they trying to kill us?"

He didn't answer. It was taking all his focus just to keep the truck on the road. The car closed the gap behind them. "I can't outrun him." He risked a quick look at her terrified face. "I'm going to try something. Hold on." Without warning he slammed on the brakes. The smaller car crashed into them from behind and ricocheted off the truck's heavy metal bumper. It skidded sideways and slid into the rocks on the roadside.

Booker pushed the truck faster to put more distance between them. A half mile down the road there was still no sign of their pursuer. He looked at Anita. "We lost them for the moment."

She managed a nod and pulled out her satellite phone. "I'm going to call Sergeant Williams."

"Yeah." While Anita fiddled with the phone, he tried to make sense of it. The guy didn't happen on them accidentally. He'd known they were here, and he had been watching and waiting.

For what?

Was it the same people who'd trashed Drew's place? Slashed Anita's tires? What were they after?

Anita finished dialing and held the phone to her ear.

An engine roared and Booker saw the car shoot out from a side trail. He had time only to call a warning to Anita before the car struck the front side bumper and pushed them over the side into the dry creek bed.

Though it was a useless effort, he kept his hands on the wheel as the truck rolled and pitched, slamming into boulders and releasing showers of gravel. They careened at a dizzying pace down the embankment until they hit the bottom with a violent smack. The truck rolled twice more and came to rest, right side up, bits of broken windshield showering down on them.

He gulped in air. "Anita?"

She was turned away from him, face leaning against the door frame.

"Anita?" He reached out a hand. "Anita? Answer me."

At his touch, she slid toward him, face bleeding from a cut on her forehead, eyes closed.

His stomach tensed. He tried to ease her gently down on the seat without moving her too much. Her eyes fluttered open and then closed again. "It's okay, honey. You're okay." He tried to find her satellite phone. It was probably on the floor near her feet. He eased out of the truck, ignoring the pain in his shoulder and made his way around to the passenger side. With fumbling fingers he found the phone.

Anita was stirring now, sighing as she struggled to consciousness. "What…?"

"We've been in an accident. I'm calling for help. Lie still."

Thanking God for the blessing of moonlight, he began to dial Williams's number.

Worry for Anita coursed through him. If she was badly hurt…
He clenched his jaw. She would be fine. She was just dazed.

Her eyes flickered open. She looked at him with an expression that changed from confusion to horror.

He did not have time to turn before something struck him in the head and his knees buckled.

Anita opened her eyes to see a masked figure loom up behind Booker and bring a bat down on his head. She tried to sit upright but before she could manage it, the assailant reached into the car and rolled her roughly onto her stomach.

Fear coiled inside her. Was she going to be assaulted? Was Booker dead from the blow to his head? A weight pressed down on her from behind. She felt the attacker rooting around in the car searching for something, heard a gasp as he or she knocked against the door frame.

Then abruptly the weight was lifted. She heard the attacker scrabbling up the slope and the distant sound of a motor. He was gone.

She pulled herself out of the car and knelt next to Booker. He lay on his side, face pale in the moonlight.

"Booker." Murmuring his name, she put her face close to his. Taut with terror, she willed her hands to stop shaking as she put her fingers to his throat. A pulse beat softly. The relief was so great that it took the last bit of strength out of her. She put her cheek against his and cried. "You're alive. Thank you for being alive." She pressed a kiss to his temple and listened to his breathing to convince herself she had not been mistaken.

The gravity of the situation took over. Booker was alive, but he might not be for long if she didn't get help. She eyed the toppled truck. No way to use that. She could call the police, but who knew how long it could take for them to get an ambulance to this remote corner of the ranch? Still, the phone seemed to be the only option.

Ignoring the pounding in her head, she desperately searched

the truck for the satellite phone. It was nowhere to be found. Thinking it might have been thrown from the vehicle, she scanned the ground outside, littered with broken glass.

No phone. It was probably tossed in the back somewhere.

Then it hit her. No camera, either. Their attacker knew exactly what he was looking for before he rammed them. He knew they had Drew's camera, and he was willing to kill them to get it back.

Her body prickled with goose bumps. He'd been watching them. Waiting for his chance.

She couldn't let fear take over. *God, please help me take care of Booker. Help me figure out what to do.*

Without a phone, her only option was to head for the distant lights of Robin's home and summon help.

How could she leave Booker there totally vulnerable? What if the attacker came back?

But if she didn't get help, he might not make it. The thought of losing him was unbearable.

Please, God.

Booker let out a soft moan. She brushed the gravel from his hair. "It's okay. I'm going to get help. I'm going to get you out of this mess."

The mess he was in because of her. Again.

She put the guilt aside and unzipped her jacket, settling it as best she could around his broad shoulders.

Then she kissed him one more time and headed off into the darkness.

In her search of the truck she'd managed to find a flashlight. She turned it on, picking her way as fast as she could over the ground. Mentally calculating, she put the ranch house about two miles away. The darkness closed around her as a cloud drifted across the moon. A sound like wet fingers squeaking across glass made her tense. Coyotes. An answering call from atop a rock formation confirmed it. There were several. This was their home.

And she was the intruder now.

A dip in the trail made her stumble and go down on one knee. For the first time she noticed how sore her back muscles felt from the crash as she straightened. Though there was no human noise, it was far from quiet, the hum of millions of night insects playing in the gloom. The bats would be active now, she thought idly, as she pictured them streaming out from their quiet caves to feed.

It comforted her somehow, knowing that the peaceful creatures were carrying out their ancient rhythm. A movement on the path in front of her made her stop. A black shape wriggled along out of her flashlight beam. A fat beetle.

She carefully stepped around it and quickened her pace as much as she dared, trying not to think of Booker lying helpless on the ground.

She had to get help.

A distant glow of headlights shone in the distance.

Her heart pounded. The assailant had come back to finish the job.

She frantically scanned the area, looking for a place to hide.

There was nothing but the flat ground, dotted with low-lying shrubs and dry grass.

The lights came closer, cutting off her route to the house.

Her thoughts whirled in circles until one took over her mind. She had to protect Booker. Even if it meant neither of them survived, she would protect him with her last ounce of strength.

Whirling around, she ran back toward the wreck, feet skidding on the gravel, stumbling over rocks. The headlights continued to close in as she raced along, wondering what she could use to protect them. The attacker had taken his bat with him. Maybe there was something in the truck—a stick, a knife, anything she could use.

She saw the truck and Booker lying next to it. Sprinting now, she raced over, rifling through the truck in search of a weapon. She found nothing.

In the back of the truck, secured by bungee cords, was a large toolbox containing a tire iron.

"Yes," she cried, as she grabbed it and made her way back to Booker.

He'd thrown off the jacket. Now his head moved and she heard him groan.

She put a hand on his forehead. "Booker."

His eyes flew open. "What…?"

"Someone rammed us and hit you over the head. I think he's on his way back."

He blinked several times and tensed.

She tried to quiet him. "Stay still. You're hurt." She squeezed the tire iron.

The headlights were almost upon them, the harsh glare making Anita squint.

Booker reached out a hand. His voice was no more than a harsh croak. "Anita, don't. Run. Get away from here."

"I'm not leaving you."

He tried again to touch her. She took his cold fingers in hers and squeezed. "It's going to be okay," she said over the hammering of her heart.

Booker lifted his head, his face drawn with pain. "No, Anita. Run."

The headlights stopped and a door opened. Anita could not see the figure that emerged through the glare of the lights.

"You're not going to hurt him again," she shouted. "I'm ready for you this time."

She heard a voice and then the headlights were extinguished, leaving Anita blinded by the sudden change. She gripped the tire iron tighter and tensed, straining to make out a silhouette.

Two flashlights were switched on and a familiar female voice called out. "What is going on here?" Robin came close enough for Anita to see her clearly.

Anita's knees almost buckled in sheer relief. For a moment,

she could not find her voice. Robin hurried over and knelt at Booker's side. Her fingers danced over his face. She called to Carlos, who was examining the truck, "Call for an ambulance." She looked up at Anita. "What happened?"

"Someone came out of nowhere and forced us off the road. After we crashed, he hit Booker with a bat." For some reason, Anita decided not to mention the stolen camera. She did not fully trust Robin, not completely, but for now the woman was the only available rescuer. "I couldn't find my phone."

Robin was silent for a moment. When she spoke it was to Carlos. "We've got to get him back to the house. It will take some time for the ambulance to make it out here and he can't be left exposed like this."

Without a word, Carlos spread a pile of blankets in the back of the pickup. He took Booker under the shoulders, and Robin and Anita hoisted his feet. They put him gently in the back of the truck. Anita hopped up next to him.

"I'll ride back here and keep him as still as I can."

Robin's eyes narrowed, but she didn't answer.

Carlos bent down and retrieved Anita's phone from the spot where it had been thrown. Robin climbed in next to Carlos, and they headed slowly back to the house. In spite of the blankets, Booker's head bounced against the truck bed. Anita gently slid his head onto her lap to cushion the blow.

He opened his eyes and groaned. "You hurt?"

She couldn't help but laugh. "No, I'm not hurt. You are. We're taking you back to Robin's house."

He raised a hand, and she took it. "Sure?"

"Yes, I'm sure. The attacker, whoever it was, didn't come back. Good thing, because I don't really know my way around a tire iron."

He smiled, his face pale in the moonlight, stained dark where the blood had dried on his forehead.

Her heart ached all over to see him hurt and vulnerable, and most of all to know his first thought was for her safety.

It's just a crazy time, Anita. Don't let your heart run away with your head.

His eyes closed again and remained that way until they arrived at the house. Gingerly they slid him from the truck and laid him on a bed in Robin's beautifully furnished guest room. Booker was moving restlessly, his eyes opening and closing.

Robin took a wet cloth Carlos provided and sponged away the blood.

Anita's stomach tensed to see how tenderly she daubed at his face. "When will the ambulance arrive?"

"Another twenty minutes, I should think."

They sat in silence for a while until a knock at the door startled them both. Carlos admitted Sergeant Williams.

The officer led Anita to the front room and jotted down the facts as Anita outlined them.

"Did you see the person's face?"

Anita sighed. "No, whoever it was wore a mask."

"Man or woman?"

"It was…" Anita stopped. She'd assumed it had been a man, but it could have easily been a woman—a strong woman. "I'm not sure."

"Tell me about the camera."

Anita related the facts about the strange pictures of text and numbers they'd seen, interspersed with the nature shots.

Williams listened. "Who knew you were going out there tonight?"

Anita kept her voice low. "Only Robin, Carlos and whomever else she told."

The back of her neck prickled as she turned to find Robin standing in the doorway.

"I can assure you, I had nothing to do with this, nor did any of my people." Robin brushed the long hair away from her face. "Booker is conscious now and trying to get out of bed. Perhaps you can talk some sense into him, since he was here because of your situation?" There was a challenge in her dark eyes.

Anita walked past her into the bedroom. Booker was awake, struggling to sit up, his face tight with pain.

"Lay down," she commanded. "You've already been moved too much for someone with a head injury."

"I'm fine." He got an elbow under him. "Nothing serious."

She planted a hand on his chest. "No, you're not. You need to go to the hospital."

"I need to get out of this bed."

Anita pushed him down. "Listen to me. You've got to get an X-ray for that stubborn head of yours. If it's clear, you'll be on your way home—but you're going to have that X-ray if I have to take you there myself."

He stopped moving and stared at her. She thought she saw the corner of his mouth move in a smile. "You're kind of small to hog-tie a guy like me, aren't you?"

Robin spoke from the doorway. "Yes, she is, but I will gladly help her."

Anita was relieved to have Robin in her corner for this one.

Sergeant Williams joined them. "And I'd have to lend them a hand, too."

His gaze traveled over the three women. With a sigh, he sank back down on the bed. "I think I'd rather take my chances with the guy and the bat."

Anita laughed. "That's a very wise choice."

Shortly the ambulance arrived, and a very irate Booker suggested staggering to the vehicle himself. "No one is carrying me anywhere," he snapped.

The paramedics cheerfully ignored him as they put him on a stretcher.

Williams offered to give Anita a ride to the hospital. She started to head out into the darkness when Robin stopped her.

"This thing between you and Booker. Is it love?"

Anita stared into Robin's elegant face. Love? The word sent her into a panic. Not love. She promised, vowed, burned it into her heart there would be no love after Jack. That was why she ran from Rockridge. And from Booker. "Booker is a friend. He's helping me find my brother. That's all." She hated the look of satisfaction that swept over Robin's face.

"Good. I will see you at the hospital in a little while."

Anita groaned inwardly. She had a feeling it would not be the last time she'd see Robin Hernando.

TEN

Booker's head felt like someone had taken a two-by-four to it. Not a two-by-four, he reminded himself, a bat. He clenched his fists as he lay on the table, waiting for the results of the CAT scan, wondering exactly how much that little procedure was going to cost. He would have cut and run if it weren't for the three determined women who practically hand-delivered him to the emergency room.

Foggy details surfaced in his mind. Anita's face, worried and tense, her slight form wielding the tire iron. Run, he'd commanded her, but she hadn't. Why had she chosen to stay there with him?

She couldn't care for him; it must have been guilt over pulling him into the hornet's nest with Drew at the center. Whatever her brother had done or hadn't, the answer was on that camera. Anita told him how the assailant had taken it. The thought of someone manhandling her like that made his pulse pound. It was probably a good thing he was unconscious at the time.

Visions of his truck skidded into his mind. He hoped it wasn't totaled. There was no way he could afford a new one, and unless he kept his fledgling desert tour business going, there was going to be no feed money for the meager remnants of his herd.

The worry drove him to try to sit up, head spinning. He made it to an upright position when the doctor came in. Anita and Robin followed her.

"Looks like you've got a hard head," the doctor said, tapping her pen on the clipboard.

Anita piped up. "I'll vouch for that."

"You've got a concussion but no fracture or hematoma that we can detect."

He sighed. "Great. Then I'm going home."

"I'd recommend you stay overnight for observation."

"No, thanks. I've got a tour to lead tomorrow morning."

The doctor frowned. "Does this involve driving?"

Booker nodded cautiously.

"I'm sorry. I'm going to insist that you don't drive, at least for twenty-four hours."

He stared at her. "Sorry, Doctor. I've got to make a living."

"No, *I'm* sorry, Mr. Scott. You cannot drive for twenty-four hours. It's not just for your safety, but for the passengers and other drivers, as well. Until the swelling in your brain eases up a bit, it is not safe."

He would have slammed his fist down on the table if it didn't hurt so much to move. No driving, no tour, no feed. He tried to think of what he could sell to make up the difference. Nothing left worth selling except what was in the little box in his dresser drawer. He couldn't let go of that, not yet.

Resignedly he nodded and the women departed while he eased on his shirt. Robin was gone when he made it to the waiting room. Anita shot to her feet, looking nervous.

"Sergeant Williams brought the loaner from the ranch. I'll drive you back."

"Gotta go see about my truck."

"Robin said she'll have it towed out first thing in the morning." Anita pointed to the clock. "It's almost one a.m. now. No sense driving all the way out there. Let me take you home."

He nodded, too tired to argue. When they were out on the road, he felt her looking at him.

"Booker, I'm really sorry about all this."

"Yeah, me, too."

"I've been thinking about what I can do to help."

He raised an eyebrow. "Why would you want to? You've got your brother to find. That's where your effort should be. I'll get along okay."

"But you need to lead that tour tomorrow. I know it's important to you."

He looked out the window at the harsh landscape, painted in luminous silver moonlight. "I'll manage somehow."

"You can't drive."

"I know," he snapped. "The doctor made that painfully clear."

"But I can."

He swiveled his head so fast a burst of pain shot up his neck. "What?"

Tangles of curly hair bobbed around her face in the warm wind from the open window.

"I can drive on your tour tomorrow. I can drive, you can navigate, we can make it work."

He was struck speechless. Why would she do this? He'd decided she was a coldhearted, arrogant woman, and the kindness of the offer, as well as her brave attempts to protect him after the wreck, confused him. "You don't have to do that."

She gave him a strange look. "I want to. It's the least I can do."

Guilt. Guilt was the reason, nothing more. His heart sank as his mind tried to think it out. If he could just make good on his tour, it would buy him some time. It was about the only thing he could buy, he thought ruefully. It would only be a Band-Aid fix, but anything that helped him hold on to the ranch for a little while longer was worth considering.

"What about Drew?"

She looked away. "Your tour is at ten. I'll have time to meet with the police in the morning. Williams said she'd brief me on their progress, so maybe I'll get a new idea where to look."

He saw her swallow hard against the desperation she must

have felt about her brother. "Listen, I'm sorry I let him get the camera. Should have seen that coming."

She shook her head. "No one could have seen that coming."

Ace barked and ran to the car as Anita pulled up. He sniffed at Booker, whining, waiting for his head scratch.

"Sorry, boy, bending is not in the cards tonight."

Anita laughed and knelt on the graveled ground, giving the dog a thorough rubdown. Ace flopped onto his back and enjoyed a belly scratch.

Booker couldn't help smile at the two of them. "Some watchdog."

Without warning, Ace leaped to his feet, ears swiveling, tail erect. He stared at the dark horizon. It took Booker a moment to spot them, the distant flicker of lights that danced against the rugged black rocks.

His stomach lurched. They were trying it out, testing the landscape and escape route. It would not be long now before they made him an offer. He felt Anita's gaze on him.

Her face seemed to shine with its own light. "What is it?"

"Nothing."

"Ace doesn't seem to think it's nothing."

The dog started to bark, the sound ringing loud through the night.

"No, Ace."

At the sharp tone from his master, the dog tapered off into a dissatisfied whine.

Anita touched his arm. "Are they trespassing?"

"Yes, but they're just moving through."

"Who?"

"Who knows? Probably nothing to worry about." Though he turned away from her, he knew she did not buy his story for a second.

"I'll be here tomorrow morning for the tour."

He could hear it in her voice, the suspicion that he was hiding something. "Don't think it's safe for you to be driving by yourself after what happened. Finished the cabin last season. It'd be a good idea for you to stay there." He held his breath, wondering if she'd see reason.

To his surprise, she nodded. "Okay. I'm too tired to drive back to the hotel tonight, anyway."

Not wanting to risk any further conversation, he nodded and led her to the small wood-sided cabin on the acreage behind the property. It was close enough that he would be able to hear any disturbance. Thinking about the intruders that even now were silently marching over his property, he wasn't satisfied.

"Mind a four-legged roommate?"

She blinked. "You want Ace to stay with me?"

"If you don't mind. We built this place for Pops's brother to stay when he visited. Ace has fond memories here because Uncle Vic made his own jerky. Ace used to come roll around on the ground long after Vic left to enjoy the smell."

Anita smiled. "I don't know anything about making jerky, but Ace is welcome."

Booker hid his sigh of relief and waited until both Ace and Anita made their way inside and he heard the sound of the bolt sliding into place. Then he allowed himself to give in to the fatigue and worry as he slowly made his way back to the house.

Inside the cabin, Anita should have been too exhausted to move. Instead her mind rode in turbulent waves. She felt like a tiny leaf in a storm, tossed helplessly in every direction. Someone wanted to stamp out every trace of her brother, right down to stealing his camera, and so far whoever it was had the upper hand. No word from Drew, and now no clues to follow. She knew she was racing against the clock to rescue him, but she had no idea which way to start running.

And then there was Booker. He knew without a doubt who was trespassing on his property, yet he made no move to stop them or call the police. Why was he covering for them? Was it Feria's people? Were they using Booker's property to smuggle drugs with his permission? The thought made her breath catch.

She tried to focus on her surroundings to take her mind off the wretched idea. Ace followed her as she moved through the place. The cabin was small, room enough for a twin bed, a bedside table and a braided rug. A collection of *Field and Stream* magazines was piled on an old wooden crate. In one corner was tiny kitchenette with a single burner, minifridge and sink. She stopped there to find a bowl and fill it with water for Ace.

A door opened onto a miniscule bathroom with a shower and a sink. It was decorated with steel-blue towels and a framed picture of the ranch. She returned to the front room.

The window looked out on a pine deck that faced the main house. She could imagine Booker and his father sitting on the front porch, talking with Uncle Vic as he smoked the jerky. She knew family was precious to Booker, especially his beloved Pops. How it must have crushed him when Pops moved to a home.

An idea kindled in her brain. Maybe if he could get the ranch back on its feet, he could afford to hire a nurse and bring his father home. The enthusiasm died when she remembered she'd made it even more unlikely for that to happen by barring him from working his mine.

Anita, you did it to protect the bats. There was no other choice.

Or was there? Had she really looked at ways to mitigate the threat or simply shut him down to cut him out of her life? To make herself an enemy instead of confronting the frightening feelings for Booker that grew every day she spent in Rockridge?

She sighed so loudly Ace trotted over and sat at her feet.

She stroked his soft ears. "Ace, I've made a complete mess of things. Did you ever feel like that?"

He wagged his tail and stared at her with brown eyes full of adoration. She kissed the top of his head and walked closer to look out into the star-spattered night. There were no more mysterious lights in the distance, no movement except for the flutter of an owl against the moonlight. But there were very real dangers out there, she knew. Feria, or their attacker.

She remembered Sergeant Williams's words. *This is a dangerous town. Very dangerous.*

With a shudder, she drew the curtains before she made up the bed with sheets Booker had set out and crawled under the covers. She noticed a Bible in a nook of the bedside table.

Her fingers sought the smooth cover, the gilt-edged pages ruffling in the silence. She remembered her mother reading aloud to her and Drew as they tucked themselves in bed and listened to her quiet voice.

And we know that in all things God works for the good of those who love Him, who have been called according to His purpose. Romans 8:28.

She felt again the excruciating pain. "How could good come out of your death, Mama? And Daddy's? Since you were killed, I've lost my way and…and hurt people who didn't deserve it. And now Drew's gone." Tears flowed down her face and soaked into the cotton pillowcase.

Lord, help me find the good in this, because right now all I see is darkness.

Ace hopped onto the foot of the bed and added his comforting weight.

She closed her eyes.

She woke before sunrise and enjoyed a brief shower. Having no change of clothes, she put on the jeans torn at the knee and ragged from her previous night's adventures. Ace waited at the door as she found her keys and headed to the loaner truck.

Better get out of here before Booker decides it's not safe for me to be driving around alone. She discouraged Ace from jumping in next to her. "You've got to keep an eye on Booker. If he tries to drive anything, you knock him over, okay?" The dog wagged his tail and watched her as she drove away toward town.

Would there be any news of her brother? She didn't think so. She'd given the sergeant strict orders to call her day or night if anything came to light. The predawn gray melted into a soft gold before it exploded across the horizon. Cliffs that paralleled the road rose in showy splendor against the bank of pearlescent clouds. For a moment, it took her breath away. She could understand why Booker made his life here, why he was so desperate to keep his corner of the desert.

Desperate enough to fall in with a drug runner? She shivered, in spite of the increasing warmth.

At the police station, the sergeant gestured for her to approach the desk, which now looked twice as full of files and papers as it had the first time Anita visited. She took a seat opposite the officer.

"Thanks for coming by, Ms. Teel."

There was little expression on the woman's face, but Anita thought she saw a hint of regret in the brown eyes. "What is it?"

"Some information has come to light."

At that moment, the door burst open and Cyrus Leeman stalked in. He carried a stack of file folders in his arms. He stopped for a moment when he saw Anita, then continued his march toward Williams's desk. "Ms. Teel, I didn't expect to see you here. I'm sorry to be the bearer of bad news."

Her stomach tightened. "What news?"

He put the stack on the desk. "Your brother's been skimming money, embezzling from *Wild World Magazine*." He smacked a hand on top of the folders. "I found some inconsistencies in here that someone worked hard to hide. A phony account with money taken every month, in odd amounts so as not to raise suspicion. It amounted to quite a sum, even in the few months I've examined." His eyes blazed.

Anita stood, ramrod straight. "My brother is only a photographer. How did he get access to your bookkeeping accounts, Mr. Leeman?"

Leeman shifted slightly, looked down at the desktop. When he raised his chin again, there was a slight flush across his pinched cheeks. "It's hard for me to say it, but he and my wife, Heidi, seemed to be spending a lot of time with each other. Heidi is the bookkeeper for my company."

She almost felt pity for the man at the hurt that showed on his face. "I don't believe what you are implying and your evidence doesn't prove anything about my brother. Let's talk to your wife, Mr. Leeman, and we'll straighten it all out."

His eyes burned into hers. "Yes, I believe that would prove your brother's guilt quite nicely. But the fact is I don't know where my wife is at the moment. She told me last week she was going to visit her sister—only I've just found out she never arrived. So your brother and my wife disappeared at the same time. You're an intelligent woman, Ms. Teel. You can't think that's a coincidence."

She kept her chin up. "I don't know what happened to my brother, or your wife, but I am not going to condemn either one until we talk to them both."

Sergeant Williams nodded. "We've got people looking for Mrs. Leeman."

"Did they check the airport? You know I found plane tickets Heidi bought for herself and Teel."

Anita was glad she'd been warned about this fact by Paul Gershwin. She directed her comment to Williams. "They didn't use them, did they?"

"No, neither one showed up at the airport. We're checking other flight information and rental car companies to see if there was a last-minute change in plans."

Leeman's face was red now. "The plan was they stole from me and ran away together," he shouted.

Anita did not back off. "My brother's wrecked motorcycle was found, and I got a phone call from him saying he was in trouble. *And* someone nearly killed Booker Scott and me for getting too close to the truth. There's more to this situation than whatever was between my brother and your wife."

A vein pulsed on Leeman's forehead. He leaned close to Anita. "Well, you better hope that if your brother is alive, you find him before I do."

Sergeant Williams stepped between them. "That's enough, Mr. Leeman. I think you'd better leave now."

He did, turning on his heel and slamming out the station door.

Anita collapsed in the chair.

Williams resumed her seat at the desk. "You okay?"

She nodded. "Did you tell him about the camera?"

"No. We haven't finished looking into that completely. I've got to go over the evidence collected from the crash site, the blind, that kind of thing."

"How bad does this look for my brother?"

She met Anita's eyes. "Honestly, not good."

Anita wanted to scream and pound on the desk. "What can I do to help find him?"

"Try to remember if there's anything he might have told you, or something odd you noticed when you were here in the spring."

"That's all?"

She sighed. "That's all."

Anita heaved herself to her feet. "I've got to get back to the ranch." She made it to the door before she turned back. "Sergeant Williams, do you think my brother is innocent in all this?"

Her silence said everything.

ELEVEN

Booker was relieved to see the truck drive back onto the property. His plans to get up and accompany Anita were foiled when she managed to sneak out before he woke. He'd found a hungry Ace sitting on the porch, ready for kibble.

"Hey, Ace. Why'd you let her get away? You're supposed to have my back."

The dog poked a wet nose against his leg. He took a deep breath. His temple pounded fiercely with every turn of his head. Nonetheless, he'd spent the past quarter of an hour packing up supplies for the tour, fully intending to drive in spite of the doctor's orders.

When Anita approached, he saw on her face that things hadn't gone well at the station. Mentally he kicked himself for not being there with her. He pulled open the door.

"Morning. I scrambled some eggs, made some bacon."

She walked past him into the kitchen and stood there, looking at the table without seeming to see it. There was an un-accustomed slump to her shoulders, a look of dejection that he hated to see.

Giving in to impulse, he put down the papers he was holding and gently wrapped his arms around her from behind. She relaxed into his embrace, letting her head fall back against his chest. He pressed his face to her hair, closing his eyes against the pleasure of having her so close.

Suddenly she turned and buried her face in his shirt, her body racked with sobs. "It's getting worse and worse. I feel like I'll never find him."

He squeezed her tighter. "We'll get through it." He was surprised to hear the word *we* come so easily from his mouth. *There is no* we. *The* we *did not work out for a reason, remember?* Pulling her to arm's length, he wiped the tears from her cheeks. "Sit down and tell me what happened."

She told him about the encounter with Leeman. "Could Drew really have been stealing? Having an affair with Leeman's wife?"

Booker considered for a moment. "What do you think?"

She shook her head vehemently, sending the dark curls dancing across her face. "No. That's not my brother."

"Okay, then. You know him better than anyone, and if you say that's how it is, then I believe it."

The smile that lit her face was nothing short of dazzling. His heart sped up.

She leaned over and kissed him on the cheek. "Thank you, Booker."

His face tingling where her lips had touched, he forced himself to walk away and fix her a plate of breakfast. "Nothing to thank me for." They sat and ate. "Listen, I'm feeling okay this morning. Slight headache is all. I think—"

She cut him off. "Don't even go there, Mr. Scott. I'm driving and you're not. When do we leave?"

He swallowed the frustration. "We're meeting the couple in front of the hotel in forty-five minutes. My buddy loaned us a Jeep."

She nodded, taking a deep drink of coffee. "Okay then, Mr. Tour Guide. Let's get on with it."

He was left holding a plate, watching as she marched out to the truck.

The older couple was decked out in full tourist regalia, visors, camera, water bottles secured to the fanny packs around their waists.

"Norm and Jackie," the man announced, shaking Booker's hand and gently squeezing Anita's fingers. "We live in Maine, so this desert thing is new to us, but I saw a bit of the hottest Africa has to offer when I served in the navy."

Booker got them settled into the backseat of the borrowed Jeep. He climbed into the passenger seat, feeling again the frustration of not being behind the wheel.

"Mr. Scott," Norm boomed as they took off. "Are we going to have trouble with the weather today?"

Booker shot a glance at the wall of clouds he'd been tracking since they left the ranch. "Maybe this afternoon. We're getting a few summer storms this month. Let's see what we can cover before the front comes in."

Jackie fingered her camera nervously. "I don't want to ruin my camera."

"If things look bad, we'll head for shelter." Booker gave Anita directions and they set off.

He tried to keep the commentary light as they drove along. The couple was enthusiastically snapping pictures of everything. They were particularly excited to get a photo of the tiny kangaroo rat making its twitchy way across the ground.

"It never needs water," Booker enthused. "Gets all the moisture it requires from the food it eats."

They drove to the mouth of a canyon, a giant saguaro cactus standing sentinel outside. Jackie and Norm were happy to exit the Jeep and explore the sheltered canyon, bathed in shadow from the massive rock walls.

"I've heard these things are protected," Norm said, looking up at the prickled sides of the saguaro.

"You heard right." Booker leaned his head back to look at the top. "Grow from a seed the size of a pinhead and only increase a quarter inch a year, if nothing happens to disturb them."

"A quarter inch?" Norm whistled. "Then this thing must be hundreds of years old." He took several pictures.

Anita joined Booker in his study of the giant cactus as Jackie and Norm wandered off a short way to take more pictures. "You know a lot about cacti."

"Think they're amazing."

She laughed. "I do, too, but mostly because they provide the nectar for the bats I study. Why do they fascinate you?"

He shrugged. "They survive in the harshest climate in the world and plenty of desert critters depend on them." He watched a small bird land gently on the prickled top. "And because they're so strong and so delicate at the same time." *Like you.* He was surprised by his own realization. When had he become such a deep thinker? The blow to his head must have shaken something loose.

He knew he was lying to himself. Her presence stirred him inside with a mixture of longing and fear. Since she'd landed in Rockridge, his heart was awash in the old feelings again, frightening, unmentionable feelings that would only result in another heartbreak.

She moved closer, and he wondered for a split second if she felt them, too.

The scream pierced Anita to the core. It took her a moment to realize the sound came from Jackie. The woman stood rigid with fear, her hands pressed together. Booker had already sprinted toward her by the time Anita got her own feet to move.

She made it to Jackie's side and saw the cause of her terror. Norm stood with his back to the canyon. Three feet in front of him was a diamondback rattlesnake, coiled and tense, tail vibrating.

Though Norm didn't speak, his face was pale, sweat beading on his forehead.

Booker edged closer. "Anita, take Jackie away from here."

She tried to move her, but Jackie was rigid with fear.

"Come with me, Jackie. Booker will help Norm."

"I can't move," she whispered. Her fingers were clenched in white knuckled terror.

They both watched Booker as he edged toward the snake.

"Norm, the snake just wants to get back to the shelter of the rocks. It's not interested in biting you. The rattles are to scare you off."

Norm nodded very slightly.

"So here's what we need to do. I'm going to go this way, to draw his attention. You move slowly away from the rocks. Slowly, do you understand? Rattlesnakes can't hear, but they sense heat and vibration. Move suddenly and he'll strike. Got it?"

Norm nodded again.

Anita watched with her heart in her throat as Booker sidled a few feet away. The snake's wedge-shaped head stayed high in the air, tongue flicking in and out. It seemed uncertain for a moment, until it shifted its attention to Booker.

Norm slowly inched away from the rocks.

Anita thought the snake had lost interest in Booker until, in one rush of movement, the snake exploded toward him, biting quickly.

With a cry she started to run to Booker, but he held up a hand and she watched in fascination as the snake slid noiselessly back under the rocks.

Booker was bent over when she reached his side. "Did it bite you?"

He didn't answer.

Norm jogged up. "How bad? I called for help. How bad, young man?"

Booker straightened, a slight grin on his face. "Good teeth." He held up a booted foot and they saw the neat holes from a set of fangs cut through the denim of his jeans. "But they only made it through my pants."

Anita felt the breath whoosh out of her.

Booker laughed. "Can't beat a good pair of cowboy boots. Haven't met a rattlesnake yet with fangs that strong."

They laughed together until Anita noticed that Jackie was not with them. She'd sunk down to her knees on the hot earth. Anita ran to her and put an arm around the woman's shoulders. Her skin felt cool and shivers shook her body.

"She's in shock," Booker said. He and Norm gently picked her up and moved her to the shade of a sprawling cottonwood tree. Anita fetched a blanket and they wrapped her in it, plying her with water to drink.

Her teeth chattered violently. "That snake. That awful snake."

Norm comforted her, and after fifteen minutes of quiet talk and back patting, a tiny stain of color returned to her face. He turned to Booker. "Sorry, son. I think this tour is over."

Anita could see the disappointment on Booker's face—and worry, too. Would Norm be inclined to pay full boat for half of a tour? She'd gotten the sense from Booker that every penny counted.

As Norm packed up his camera, a Border Patrol SUV rolled up in a cloud of dust. Anita could see Booker tense as Tony Rogelio got out.

"Got a call you had some trouble."

Booker tersely filled him in. Rogelio meandered over to talk to Norm and Jackie. When he returned, there was a sardonic smile on his lips. "Looks like they want me to take them home. Lady's pretty freaked about your snake."

Booker's jaw clenched. "Not my snake."

"Whatever. I'm taking her back." He slid a glance at Anita and his voice became smooth, soft. "Can I offer you a ride back, Ms. Teel? Looks to be a storm coming in. Wouldn't want you caught out in it."

Anita straightened, keeping her tone honey sweet. "No, thank you, Agent Rogelio."

"Call me Tony."

"Tony, then. I'm going to drive back with Booker." No need to tell him Booker was restricted from driving on his own tour. For some reason she didn't want to give the agent the satisfaction of seeing Booker in such a vulnerable spot.

Rogelio tipped his hat. "Another time, then."

She didn't answer.

"Booker, I need a word before I escort the tourists home."

Booker stiffened, but followed the agent a few yards away, out of earshot. Anita strained to pick up anything from their conversation. All she could do was read the body language: Booker, taut and angry. Rogelio, enjoying his position of power.

What were they talking about? Did he have questions about the strange nighttime activity on Booker's ranch? Did Rogelio somehow know about his connection to Feria? Whatever it was, she hated the thought that Rogelio was making Booker squirm. What about the man made her dislike him so much?

She hadn't time to form any theories as Norm helped his wife into Rogelio's SUV and handed Booker a check.

"Paid for the whole tour, son. Added a nice tip for the extra excitement. Give this old navy goat something to jaw about."

Booker's eyes were wide as he shook Norm's hand before they drove away.

Anita patted Booker on the shoulder. "You see? He was duly impressed by my awesome driving."

He laughed. "I think he was more impressed by the rattlesnake."

They climbed into the Jeep as the first drops of rain began to fall. Anita shot a worried glanced at the mass of clouds. "Is this going to be a big storm?"

Booker was thoughtful. "I'm thinking so. Let's see if we can make it a few miles toward home before it really lets loose."

Though he took a step toward the driver's side, Anita quickly cut him off and slid in. She heard his frustrated sigh. As she eased the Jeep back toward the canyon, she could contain her worry no longer.

"Booker, what's going on between you and Rogelio?"

His head snapped toward her. "What do you mean?"

"The conversation between you two. I could read the body language. You weren't happy."

He wiped a drop of rain from his cheek. "I don't like the man personally. As far as professionally, well, I'm trying to figure that out."

She remained silent, feeling like he was talking more to himself than her.

"It's like Ace. When I found him, he'd been badly beaten and dumped on the side of the road, really messed up."

She gasped in horror. "Poor Ace. Who would do that to a dog?"

He continued as if he hadn't heard her. "Took me half an hour in the pouring rain to get that dog in my truck, and I'm still surprised he didn't take a chunk out of me. I guess somehow he knew I was trying to help. Brought him home and fixed him up. Now he'd walk through fire for me or anyone I care about. But strangers? People he doesn't know well? There's always that tension in him, a sort of wariness. Guess that's how I feel about Rogelio."

He rested his head on the back of the seat and looked up at the sky. Anita guessed he must still be feeling significant pain due to the attack. She wanted to press him, to resolve in her mind what was going on in his life, but she didn't have the heart. Besides, the rain had begun to fall harder now, and although they'd stopped long enough for Booker to unroll the soft canvas top, it took all her concentration to keep the vehicle on the slick road.

The storm turned nasty, dumping the water in sheets that pounded against the car and bounced upward off the road. Thunder rolled through the clouds. Anita's hands were tense around the steering wheel.

Booker called above the noise of the storm. "Pull over here. There's an old building we can take shelter in a half mile up this road."

Anita was only too happy to comply. She drove up a steep slope until a small wooden shack came into view. They jumped out and hurried into the rickety structure.

Anita pushed the sopping hair out of her face. It was empty of any furniture except for a rusty card table, two chairs and an old file cabinet with the drawers open. Faded maps were tacked to the walls, and a shadowy hallway led off to another room in the back.

"What is this place?" Anita asked, fingering a stack of old *Field and Stream* magazines.

"Used to belong to the Department of Forestry, but they don't use it anymore. I've taken shelter here a few times, and I'm sure other ranchers have, too." He took off his jacket and sopping baseball cap. His hair stood in wet curls around his brow. He caught her smile. "What?"

"You look like a wet cat."

He laughed, low and soft. "I've looked worse."

Anita hung her jacket on a hook by the door and they sat on the hard chairs. Booker removed a thermos from his pack and poured them both some hot coffee. She should have felt awkward, sitting in the still shack with the man she'd tried desperately to forget. Instead it was pleasant, companionable and something more. She realized with a start that he was one of the few people in the world who had seen her inner emotional mess. Not all of it, though, she reminded herself. Not even Jack had seen all the damage done by the time spent with him.

She noticed Booker was gazing out the window into the sheeting rain, eyes lost in thought. "What are you thinking about?"

He shook his head. "Just trying to figure out why someone wanted Drew's camera badly enough to almost kill us for it. Do you think he took incriminating pictures of something?"

"Or someone." She sighed, and walked to the window. "The desert is so huge, so unforgiving. The chance of finding him seems like a million to one."

"Maybe he's not here anymore."

"What do you mean?"

"He could have made it out, run and holed up somewhere else."

"Why would he do that unless Leeman's right and he's guilty?"

Booker drank coffee without answering.

Anita pressed a hand to the window's cold glass.

A face loomed up out of the storm.

She screamed.

TWELVE

Booker made it to Anita's side in an instant.

She pointed a shaking finger outside.

He sprang to the door and wrenched it open, ignoring the stabbing pain in his head from the sudden movement.

Diego was half turned, ready to run. Booker grabbed him by the arm, feeling the man's fear through his sodden jacket. He hauled him inside, keeping him restrained by a firm grip on his collar.

Diego's hair was wet, plastered to his head in a black helmet. He talked in Spanish through chattering teeth. *"No quiero problemas."*

"Sit down," Booker commanded.

When Diego made no move do so, Booker propelled him into a chair.

Keeping a hand on the man's back, Booker tried to make eye contact. "Why are you here, Diego? In English."

Diego switched to heavily accented English. "I saw your Jeep coming this way. I know about this place. I use it sometimes to sleep if I can't find work." His eyes shifted toward the door.

Booker knew he would bolt if given the chance, so he sidled over to block the exit. "Why did you need to find us?"

Diego's eyes slid again to the door. Then he shrugged, hesitating for just a moment. "Looking for work."

Booker crossed his arms. "I don't think so. Try again. The real story this time."

Diego's knees bobbed up and down with nervous energy. He looked down at the puddle of rainwater that collected around his shoes. "Don't want trouble."

The man was shivering. Booker nodded to Anita, who poured some hot coffee into a paper cup and put in on the table in front of him.

Diego curled his hands around the warmth and gave Booker a quick look. "You've been good to me, given me some food when you could, not hassled me."

Sensing something else was coming, Booker didn't interrupt.

"That's why I told him I'd do it."

Anita sat next to him at the table. "Who?"

Diego grew more agitated and began to rattle off a string of Spanish. Booker couldn't follow it all, but one word jumped out at him. He could see a reaction in Anita, too.

She jerked at the word *hermano*. "You've seen my brother? When? When did you see him? Tell me."

Diego shrank back at Anita's cry. Booker put a hand on her shoulder and squeezed. "He's going to tell us everything. Let him think it through."

Diego looked at them with wary eyes. "No cops?"

"Never mind that." Anita's eyes were wild. "What do you know about my brother?"

Booker thought Anita was close to jumping across the table. "Diego is here illegally, Anita. He's got reason to avoid the cops if he can." He met Diego's worried eyes. "We will only mention your name to the cops, if we have to. I'll tell them you helped us. I give you my word."

He bobbed his chin at Anita. "Her?"

She shook her head violently. "No, of course not. I don't

want to make trouble for you, Diego. I'm only interested in helping Drew. Please tell me about my brother. Please."

He drank some of the coffee, his fingers tight around the cup. "Saw him yesterday, at night."

"So he's alive." Anita's voice trembled. "I knew it. I could feel it. Was he hurt?"

Diego nodded. "Banged up, hurt here." He pointed to his side. "He asked me for a phone, but I don't have one."

Booker could see truthfulness on the man's face, mixed with the fear. "It's okay. Go on. Tell us the rest."

"Told me he was brother to the scientist lady. Asked if she was okay. That's about all. I left pretty quick."

Anita whispered. "Where?"

"He was holed up in an equipment shed along the highway. I stay there sometimes, too. That's how I know it." He toyed with the cup for a moment. "Feria's men know it, too."

Booker felt Anita jerk. "Do they know Drew's there?"

Diego nodded. "I think so. Seen them watching."

"What else did Drew say? Did he tell you what he's running from?" Anita's shoulders were tense as steel under Booker's fingers.

Diego shook his head. "No. I don't want to know what his trouble is. He told me to find you and tell you to go home. There is too much…" Diego searched for the word. He looked at Booker. *"Es peligroso."*

Booker felt a twinge. "Dangerous. Drew thinks it's too dangerous for you to be involved." He couldn't agree more. The stakes were getting higher all the time, as the ache in his head reminded him. How much longer could he keep her safe in the middle of this mystery that got more tangled each day?

Anita shot to her feet. "Is that all? He didn't say anything about who is after him?"

Diego shook his head. "No more."

"You've got to take us there, to the place where he's staying. Please."

His eyes widened. "I don't want trouble."

"There will be no trouble," Anita said, her voice pleading. "He's my brother. Please help me find him. I'm begging you."

Booker knew it was a bad idea. They should call the cops. Whoever was out there could have followed them as easily as Diego had. Her expression made his breath catch, so hopeful, so filled with love for her brother. They were going, he knew, with no cops for backup. He tightened his jaw. So be it. If someone tried another attack, he'd be ready.

Diego exhaled softly and nodded.

They waited for the rain to let up. Anita couldn't sit. The knowledge that Drew was definitely alive filled her with a restless, unbridled joy. Whatever the trouble was, whatever he had or hadn't done, they could fight it, as long as he was alive. She paced in restless circles around the small cabin until the rain finally eased off.

She practically ran to the Jeep and headed for the driver's seat, but Booker blocked her path.

"I'm driving."

"But—"

"I'm fine. It's been long enough. You need to keep watch for him. I'm driving."

The set of his jaw told her he wasn't going to be diverted. She climbed in the passenger side and Diego hopped in the jump seat, hat pulled low over his eyes. He directed them back down to the main road.

"This way. Eight miles or so until we turn."

Anita's head swam as they rolled along. Her brother had no phone. That explained why he didn't call. But why hadn't he gone to the nearest town to find one? Maybe he was too injured to make it that far. The thought chilled her. He could have flagged down a car and asked for help. But there were few vehicles traveling this road that wound along through miles of mesquite and jimsonweed. Besides, she reminded herself, he's scared to death that someone will find him. Was it the someone who'd stolen the camera and hurt Booker?

She pulled her still-damp jacket tighter around herself.

Booker gave her a look that seemed tinged with worry. She knew he was afraid she'd be disappointed again. He had been her only support through the whole ordeal. Without thinking, she reached out a hand and squeezed his muscular arm.

A smile lit his eyes for a moment before he turned his attention back to the road.

They turned off the highway and traveled a few steep miles downhill to an area of flat brown grass dotted with unused tractors, a water tank lying on its side and a huge metal shed with rusted corners.

"What is this place?" Anita asked.

"Storage yard for a few of the smaller ranches around here. The property owners pick a spot and deposit all their gear, sort of a communal supply where you take what you need and park it here when you're done."

Diego pointed at the old shed. "There. He is hiding in there."

Anita wanted to run, but Booker put a hand on her arm.

"Let's take it slow. He's spooked as it is. We don't know what we're walking into."

She forced herself to walk, picking her way over the rocky ground toward the shed, which shimmered with moisture from the recent downpour. When they were a few feet from the door, Anita half whispered, "Drew? Are you in there?"

The only sound was the slow dripping of water from the corrugated metal roof.

She tried a little louder. "Drew. It's Ani and Booker. Are you in there?"

Still not a sound.

Booker held up a hand and gestured for her to wait. He grasped the rusted metal handle and pulled slowly. The door didn't budge. He wrapped two hands around it this time and heaved until the door slid open with a loud squeal of metal.

He crouched there, listening. Anita's heart pounded inside her with the force of a jackhammer. What would she find inside?

Booker crept in slowly, and she followed in spite of his warning look.

The interior was hot and stuffy, filled with crates of tools and an old run-down tractor in the corner. A sound of dripping water echoed loudly.

They walked softly around the piles of machinery.

"Drew," Anita half whispered again. "Are you in here?"

The only answer was the slow plop of water against metal.

She continued on. Maybe he was asleep or… She could not bear to finish the thought.

Booker called to her. "Over here, Anita."

She scrambled to him, her stomach in knots.

"Look." Booker knelt. There was a rough woolen blanket tossed on the cement floor and the remnants of a cracker, now at the mercy of a platoon of ants.

"So he *was* here." The truth of it almost took her breath away. Drew had been here, in this very spot, not long ago, alive. She scanned the space desperately. "Where has he gone? Do you think he'll be back?"

Booker continued to look around the improvised bedding. "I'm not sure. Looks like he left in a hurry." He poked at an unopened package of saltines that stuck out from under the blanket.

She swallowed hard. "Do you think someone found him here? Feria's men, maybe?"

He shook his head. "I don't know. But we'd better get the police out here."

"We promised Diego no cops."

"We'll leave him out of it."

Anita took a breath. "No."

"No?"

"No police."

"Anita—"

"I know, it would be the smart thing to do, the appropriate thing, but someone is trying to kill my brother and I'm not going to do anything to risk his life further."

He sighed and folded his arms across his broad chest. "All right, it's your call. What next?"

Desperation swelled inside her. "I don't know." The dripping was quieter now, a beam of sunlight snaking its way into the darkened shed. Something caught her eye. She inhaled sharply and sank to her knees. There on the bottom of a wood crate, was a message scrawled in black.

"Booker, he left a note."

Booker joined her on the floor and they peered at the side of the crate.

"He scratched it there with a nail. I can't make it out." Booker moved closer until his face was inches from the wood. Then he straightened with a sigh.

She grabbed his arm. "What does it say?"

"Hernando's overlook."

"Hernando? As in Robin Hernando?"

He nodded.

"She has some sort of overlook on her property."

"Yep. Been there once or twice, but it doesn't get visited much. It's off the road a bit."

Her excitement kindled higher. "Do you think that's where Drew went? He left a message to show us where to meet him?"

"No. He told Diego he didn't want you involved. This message must be for someone else. The cops, maybe? Seems strange, though. Why wouldn't Drew head to Robin's in the first place? She'd let him use the phone, if nothing else. Might even let him stay there if she knew he was a friend of Heidi's. Why come here to hole up? What's he running from?"

Anita brushed off the knees of her jeans. "I don't know, but I'm going to find out." She had almost turned away when he caught her hand.

"Anita, there's something not right about this whole thing,

something we aren't seeing." His face was shadowed, a bruise from their attack visible on his cheek.

"Are you saying I shouldn't go?"

He smiled. "I'm smart enough to know that would be like telling the rain not to fall."

His words and the concern on his face brought a smile to her own. Without thinking, she held a hand to his cheek. "You've been very good to me, and I appreciate it."

He covered her hand with his and the feel of his strong fingers wrapped around hers made her head swim. After a moment, he released her.

Anita almost ran to the exit. "Let's go tell Diego."

Booker fastened the metal doors again and looked around. "No need. He's gone."

THIRTEEN

They kept an eye out for Diego as they drove cautiously back to the main road. There was no sign of him.

"Do you think he's telling the truth?" Anita called over the sound of the rain that had returned. "Maybe he hurt my brother, took him somewhere."

Booker's gaze remained on the road. "I don't think he'd hurt anyone. He's just trying to keep out of trouble, fly under the radar. Come down to it, he didn't have to show us where Drew was holed up in the first place. Would have been easier to go about his business, not get involved."

She sighed. "I guess." She found their slow pace infuriating. It would have been so much more satisfying if Booker floored the gas pedal as they headed to Robin's ranch. It took more than an hour before they pulled into the long drive toward the elegant house.

"I don't suppose we could just drive up to the overlook? Without stopping at the house?"

Booker's brow furrowed. "You don't like Robin much, do you?"

Anita shrugged. "I just want to get to my brother as quickly as possible."

He smiled. "Doesn't pay to go trespassing on a person's property. Good way to get shot around here. We'll try to keep it short."

Robin greeted them and insisted they come in.

Anita tried to decline but Robin cut her off. "If you wish to search my property, I at least should be filled in on the whys and wherefores. Don't you think?"

She tried to squash the feelings that rose when Robin touched the bruise on Booker's face.

"You're healing well?" Her dark eyes seemed to smolder.

He nodded. "Yes. Hardheaded, like I told you."

She laughed.

Anita broke in with a hurried explanation for their visit.

"Your brother isn't here. I only know him in passing, but if he arrived in need of help, I'd certainly let him use the phone. He did not come to me for help or to hide out on my property." She looked thoughtful. "Why would he have need to hide, anyway?"

Anita didn't answer.

"Unless he is guilty of the things they are saying in town. He was, perhaps, stealing from the paper and he does not wish to meet anyone who might turn him in to the police."

"My brother is not a thief." Anita spoke more sharply than she'd intended. "I don't know what you've heard, but it's not true."

Robin nodded. "Forgive me, but I consider Heidi Leeman a friend. I have heard things, bits about your brother and his infatuation with her. These things are not helpful to Heidi and her marriage, such as it is."

Anita did not trust herself to answer without shouting. Booker stepped in.

"All we've got is rumor so far. The important thing is to find Anita's brother so he can clear things up himself. Do we have your permission to go to the outlook?"

Robin was silent for a moment. "Yes, and I'll go with you. Wait one moment while I let my staff know."

The thought of sitting in the cramped Jeep with Robin made her blood simmer, but Anita knew she couldn't very well ask the woman to stay away from a spot on her own property. She clamped her jaws together and headed out to the Jeep, sliding into the passenger seat before Robin could claim the spot.

The rain eased into a gentle patter as they drove along the main road that bisected Robin's ranch. In spite of the moisture, the air was hot and thick. Booker turned off onto a steep slope, and the Jeep bounced and heaved over the rough trail.

"What do you use the outlook for?" Anita forced herself to say.

"Nothing, really. It is quite old. My great-grandfather had a man posted there throughout the night, I'm told, to keep watch for cattle rustlers and Indian attacks. Now it is mostly unused, though your brother asked to take some photos from there while he was here for the tortoise photography."

"Did you talk with him much?"

"No. He was charming, but it was a very busy time for me then, as I recall."

Robin found her brother charming? Anita hoped Drew had not fallen under the lovely woman's spell. She imagined Robin could exert plenty of influence over the male species with one look from under her long lashes.

Anita mentally chided herself for her inexplicable dislike of Robin. *Stop being petty. Do anything to find your brother. That's what's important.* The excitement in her gut increased along with the elevation. Booker pulled the Jeep up to a steep slice of rock that jutted against the clouded sky. The spit of land was rocky and speckled by twisted trees and low-lying shrubs. Anita could just make out the start of a winding trail that snaked upward and out of sight behind a bend.

She was out of the car in a flash, headed toward the base of the trail. The newly washed ground was damp but not sticky. The cool air bathed her heated face as she climbed. She heard Booker help Robin from the car but she didn't stop. If her brother was at the top of this rocky nowhere, she was going to get to him as fast as she could manage.

As she pressed along through shrubs that sometimes crowded the path, she hoped any rattlesnakes in the area had curled up tight under their rocky shelters. She tried to keep the thought of Norm's snake encounter from her mind.

The slope was steep enough that she was breathing hard by the time she crested the top. The path emptied out onto a flat space, relatively bare except for an old wooden tower with an enclosed room at the top.

Booker called her name, a note of warning in his tone, but she took off running for the rickety ladder. He was here; she could feel it. Her brother was here.

The wood slats were old but solid as she made her way to the top. Halfway up she was startled by a bird that darted out from between two boards and flew away with a frightened trill.

Below, she could hear Booker and Robin start up after her.

The top of the ladder was only a few yards away. She hazarded a quick look around as she climbed. The view was breathtaking, a panorama of ragged cliffs and gently rolling flatland. If he'd had his camera, Drew would have taken a thousand pictures of it by now. The thought made her climb faster until she was panting from the effort.

A small door at the top stood in her way. She unlatched it and climbed onto the platform. "Drew, it's Ani," she gasped.

The space was quiet and warm. A stack of crates was lined up next to one side, along with several coils of rope. Large cardboard boxes were scattered around the space. "Drew?"

There was no answer. He was scared, keeping quiet until he found out if she'd come alone. She stepped to the center of the wooden floor. "I've got Booker with me and Robin Hernando, but that's it. No cops. We're here to help, Drew. It's okay."

Silence.

A tingle of fear began to creep into her heart. She moved quickly around the space, checking behind the crates for any sign that her brother was there. He might have heard them coming and hid. There must be some sign that he'd been here, at least. She picked her way over to the boxes and opened the first one that wasn't taped shut. It was a collection of old bridles.

She moved on to the next two but found only discarded gear and envelopes stuffed with aged pamphlets and invoices, nothing to point to her brother.

A spot of color caught her eye. She made her way around the crates to the yellow rug rolled up behind them. The rug was oddly shaped, she thought. Moving closer, her skin began to prickle and an icy hand seemed to grip her stomach.

One booted foot protruded from under a roll of wool rug.

Anita could not contain the horror that came out in a gut-wrenching scream.

Booker was several rungs from the top when he heard Anita's cry. Heart pounding, he scrambled up the rest of the ladder and crashed into the space at the top. Anita stood with her hands clamped over her mouth, eyes wild, staring at something behind a stack of crates. He ran to her and, after a quick glance, grabbed her shoulders and moved her away.

He placed her at the far end of the room by a small window. The sun streaming through the glass showed her face to be pale as paper, her whole body trembling. Robin crested the top of the ladder and stood there, panting, her eyes traveling over the space.

He motioned for Robin to join Anita and he returned to the crates.

It was a body wrapped in the wool rug, a woman's body. Her long yellow hair streamed out of one end of the roll. Booker didn't know her well, but he'd seen her enough to make an identification.

"What is it?" Robin demanded. "What is over there?"

He hesitated, fighting against his own disgust. "A woman's been killed and left here."

"Who?" Robin's eyes were round with fear. "Tell me who."

He turned away from the broken body. "I think it's Heidi Leeman."

Robin's mouth opened but she didn't speak. When she did, her voice came out as a whisper. "Not Heidi."

Booker took his phone from his pocket and dialed. His message to Sergeant Williams was brief. When he finished, he turned to them. "It would be best if you both waited in the Jeep. Do you think you can make the climb down?"

Anita took a deep breath and nodded. He was relieved to see the return of courage in her eyes. Eyeing Robin, he knew he was going to need Anita's help.

Robin stood as if she hadn't heard him. "Oh, Heidi," she whispered over and over, her eyes unfocused. "I'm so sorry, so sorry."

Anita drew Robin toward the ladder. "Let's go down. We'll help you."

Booker went first, keeping an eye on both women, praying that they would not lose their grip on the descent. He figured he could at least break their fall if they did. Robin moved like a woman in a dream. Or maybe a nightmare.

She and Heidi were friends, good friends, from what he could recall, even though Robin insisted on their earlier visit that she hadn't seen Heidi in months. Booker was no forensic expert, but he could tell Heidi Leeman had been dead only a few days. Had she been murdered right there on Robin's property?

He tried to focus on the things he could control. He helped Anita get Robin into the front seat with a blanket wrapped around her. The woman rocked gently back and forth, moaning.

Anita refused to get in the car. Instead she paced in little circles, hugging herself. Booker saw the unbearable fear on her face, and it nearly drove him crazy. What could he do to help her? The crushing disappointment of not finding her brother, compounded now by a murder, seemed too much for one person to take. Had she put it together yet? As he watched her frenzied pacing, he guessed she was puzzling over the same thing he was. Why had her brother left a note guiding them straight to a murder victim? The second part was even more unsettling. What did her brother know about Heidi's death?

Booker made sure Robin was still wrapped in the blanket and tried to talk to her again. It was no use. She stared at her hands, lips moving but no audible words coming out. He approached Anita.

"Is there anything I can get you?"

Her brown eyes fastened on his and he saw her purposefully still the tremor in her lips by pressing them firmly together. "No, thank you."

He wanted to find something hopeful in the situation, some shred that would explain any of it, but nothing came to mind. If things had looked bad for Drew before, now they were rock-bottom, and both of them knew it.

The crunch of tires announced the arrival of Sergeant Williams. She got out and spoke to them briefly before heading up the ladder with another officer and some bulky camera equipment. When she climbed back down thirty minutes later, her face was grim. She took out a notebook and approached Booker and Anita.

"Why did you come here?"

Booker remained silent. He knew what they had to do, but he did not want to be the one to force Anita into it.

Anita exhaled sharply. "We got a tip from someone that my brother was hiding in a shed."

"A tip from whom?"

Anita shook her head. "I promised I wouldn't get him involved."

Her eyes narrowed. "He's already involved, but we'll leave that for a moment. You went to the shed?"

"Yes. We couldn't find him, but we saw a message scratched into the wood that directed us here."

"Your brother wrote the message?"

Anita nodded. "I think so."

"So he knew Mrs. Leeman was dead."

She blinked several times. "It seems that way."

A gray Mercedes shot up the walkway in a shower of gravel. Cyrus Leeman bolted from the driver's seat and Paul Gershwin followed from the passenger side. Paul tried to put a restraining arm on his boss, but Leeman shook him off.

"What's going on? I heard on the scanner. Is it my wife? Have you found her?" His eyes burned with strong emotion in his pale face.

Sergeant Williams held up a hand and gestured for him to follow her away from the group. "Let's talk over here, Mr. Leeman. This is going to be a shock."

His face reddened, and he planted his feet. "I want to know now. Did you find my wife up there?"

The officer nodded. "Yes, I'm sorry. It appears your wife was murdered several days ago."

Leeman's face went slack for a moment. He took an audible breath. "Murdered. How? How did you find her?"

Anita cleared her throat and tried to talk but her voice broke.

Booker stepped slightly in front of her. "We found a message in a warehouse not far from here. We came looking for Drew."

"Drew." Leeman spat out the word. "Well, I guess you're on the right track, then. When you find him, you'll have the man who murdered my wife."

Gershwin stepped forward. "Let me take you back, Mr. Leeman. I can help you, er, with any calls you need to make."

Leeman appeared not to have heard. He glared at Anita. "My wife is dead and your brother killed her."

Booker saw Anita flinch, but she stood her ground.

"My brother is not a murderer. He was Mrs. Leeman's friend. Isn't that right, Paul?"

Gershwin nodded. "They seemed fond of each other."

"Fond? Is that what you call it when someone has an affair? I'm glad you're all painting Drew out to be such a great guy. Me? I'm not buying it. Drew was stealing from my company and cozying up to my wife to cover his tracks." Leeman looked up into the sky and shook his head. "Why didn't I see it before? Of course. Heidi figured it out, went to confront Drew and he killed her."

Booker spoke up. "We don't know that."

"It all fits. Parts of my computer system are wiped clean. I've got missing data disks that happen to be the accounting records for the past eight months. Heidi took them, intending to confront Drew. He killed her. He's a murderer."

Booker saw from the look on Anita's face that she was about to fall apart. He turned to Sergeant Williams. "I'm not going to stand here and let him attack her."

Leeman strode closer until he was inches from Booker's face. "You're going to stay out of it, like the dumb cowboy you are."

Booker stiffened and raised his chin so it just topped Leeman's head. "I don't think so. You run a magazine. You don't run this investigation and you aren't my boss."

Leeman threw a quick punch.

Booker raised an arm to ward off the blow and quickly hooked a leg behind Leeman, causing him to fall backward.

Leeman jumped to his feet and hurled himself at Booker until they both went down in a pile of arms and legs.

Leeman was smaller than Booker, but the man was crazed and Booker felt a knifing pain in his head from the earlier attack. It took several minutes for Booker to finally get the guy stomach down on the ground, one knee planted on his back. By that time, Sergeant Williams was able to help restrain him. She looked at Booker, a bead of sweat rolling down her face.

"Take the women back to the ranch house. I'll come talk to you there in a while."

Booker nodded and took a few deep breaths to control his spinning head. Anita followed him to the Jeep. They rode back to the house in complete silence.

He managed to get them both sitting down with glasses of water that neither woman touched. It wasn't the time to ask questions, so he swallowed his need to know.

Anita straightened, as if she had come to some internal decision. She leaned forward on the couch and fixed Robin with a glare.

"All right. It's just us. No cops around. It's time for you to tell the truth about Heidi Leeman."

FOURTEEN

Anita knew by the set to his chin that Booker didn't approve of her tactics or timing. She didn't care. Every moment—every second, it seemed—brought her brother closer to disaster. Now the stakes were ratcheted up by the murder, a murder she was sure her brother had no part of.

Robin blinked and stared at her. "I don't know what you mean."

"Yes, you do. You said you hadn't seen Heidi here in months, but I think that's a lie. I think she was here recently, and I think when the cops come here I'll tell them about the hairbrush in your guest bath. I'll bet when they run the DNA tests they find out that's Heidi's hair."

Robin's mouth opened. "I—"

"Tell the truth." Anita allowed her voice to soften a bit. "I know you were friends. You need to tell us for her sake, too."

Robin shuddered. When she spoke, her voice was low. "Yes, she was my friend, a dear friend, perhaps a sister, even. She was having trouble, so she asked me to let her stay here for a few days, and she asked for my discretion."

Booker shifted on the chair. "What kind of trouble?"

"Marital trouble. Cyrus is a controlling man, a possessive person, and she wanted out. She decided it would be easiest to pretend she was going to visit a relative, but instead she came here to rest and arrange things for her escape to Mexico."

"Why not just confront him? This is not the Dark Ages. People get divorced all the time."

She shook her head. "She was afraid of him, afraid of his temper. She knew as soon as she mentioned divorce he would freeze their assets and try to take even the inheritance she'd been given by her father. It would be an ugly battle, so she decided to try to put things in order without his knowledge."

"So you took her in. Then what happened?"

Robin shrugged. "We had a lovely time, watching old movies, cooking together, painting our nails. Like sisters would." A tear rolled down her face. "Then she arranged to go. I expected her for one final breakfast before she left—but when she didn't come, I assumed she left a bit early. Never would I have imagined…right on my own property."

Anita handed her a tissue and gave her arm a squeeze. "I'm sorry. So sorry." She waited a moment for the woman to control herself before she asked the next question. "What about the embezzlement situation? Did she ever talk about that?"

"No, but she spent plenty of time on her laptop. She downloaded lots of files to disks but she didn't say what it was about. It worried her, though. I could tell. She insisted she did not want me involved in whatever it was."

Booker spoke gently. "When the police come, you can tell them and they'll search for the disks."

She nodded.

Anita cleared her throat and asked the question she was most afraid of. "Robin, did my brother ever come here? When Heidi was staying over?"

Robin looked her full in the face. "Yes, he did. Twice. They talked outside, with much emotion, but I did not hear what they said. Heidi told me Drew was helping her with a business problem. She begged me not to tell anyone he was here."

Anita felt the walls close in around her. "Tell me one more thing, please. Did Heidi seem scared of my brother?"

Robin let out a long sigh. "I did not think so, but she was scared of someone, and that someone probably killed her."

Anita could not think of a single thing to say. Silence filled up her mind and soul. *Help me, God,* was all she could manage as the police arrived to begin the questioning.

Williams and her team found no disks, or laptop or anything else that would lead them to solving the riddle. Booker drove Anita back to the hotel. He'd insisted she stay in his tiny cabin, and Anita didn't have the will or the courage to defy him. Instead she'd packed a bag and let him deliver her back to his ranch. The late-afternoon sun shone a deep gold as they drove up, and though the afternoon was sweltering, she could not shake an inner chill. Ace barked a hello and raced to greet them.

She knelt and buried her face in his fur, listening to the thump of his heart. She thought he understood somehow, the turmoil that rolled inside her, the helplessness that paralyzed her. When she released him and started to cry, Ace sat pressed to her thigh, occasionally licking the salty tears from her cheek. She felt Booker crouch next to her.

"I'm such a mess…I'm sorry… Something about the dog kind of set me off."

He laughed softly, smoothing her hair. "I know. He's a good listener, even when you aren't talking. Come inside and let's have some dinner."

She wiped her face and followed him into the house, Ace keeping close by her side.

They ate sandwiches without much conversation until Anita couldn't stand it anymore. "I think Drew wanted the police to find Heidi. He knew she'd been murdered. That's why he left the note."

Booker chewed thoughtfully. "Could be. Do you think he knows who killed her?"

"Yes. That's part of the reason he's staying in hiding. Do you think Diego could find him again?"

"I don't think we're going to see much of Diego anymore after we told the police he led us to Drew's hideout. Even though we didn't give them his name, they'd still like to talk to him, and he definitely doesn't want to talk to them."

"I hope we didn't get him in trouble."

"He'll be all right. He knows how to get around okay."

The phone rang and Booker picked it up. "Scott." He listened, his brows furrowing. "I'll get it to you by the end of the week."

Anita turned her eyes to her dinner and tried not to eavesdrop. Booker's anxious tone came through, anyway, though he moved as far away as the cord would allow.

"I know it's late. I'll get it to you, I promise."

Anita's stomach spasmed at the desperation in his voice.

"By tomorrow, then." Booker hung up the phone and stared at it for a moment, unmoving.

Anita spoke quietly. "Is everything okay?"

He sighed, a low sound that seemed to come from deep inside. "Electric company. Payment's late. They get their money tomorrow or we lose our power."

"Oh."

Booker scrubbed his hands over his face. "When Pops was here in the summer, he couldn't take the heat. Stayed inside and we kept the air running twenty-four/seven. Killed us on the utility bill so we only paid half." He grimaced. "They want their other pound of flesh."

She toyed with her napkin. "I, um, I have some money you could borrow, just to get you through this rough patch."

His face flushed. He opened his mouth to speak and turned away instead, to look out the window.

She feared she'd made a terrible mistake.

When he turned back, his face was in control. "I appreciate that. Thank you, but I'll manage."

She nodded. "Yes, I'm sure you will."

He fisted his hands on his hips. "Can't help wondering, though."

"What?"

"How come this time you're helping, when your last visit you tried your best to shut me down?"

The heat rose in her face. "I wasn't trying to shut you down."

"Not the way I saw it."

Her heart spoke the truth over the pride. She had tried to shut him down, in more ways than one. She'd told herself it was to protect the bats. Did he know the truth? She got up from the table and took her plate to the sink to buy some thinking time.

She steeled her spine. "I did the right thing. But I may have gone about it the wrong way."

He stared at her. "Partnering with Leeman was definitely the wrong way."

She faced him, chin up. "I didn't realize Leeman had an agenda until I came back here. He used me."

"And you let him."

She huffed. "Yes, I guess I did. What does Leeman want with your land, Booker? You never bothered to tell me."

His eyes blazed. "You never bothered to ask. I was busy thinking about other things, like us."

Her cheeks burned. It wasn't because she hadn't wanted to know every detail about his life. How could she explain her love for him and the fear it ignited deep in her heart? A fear that made her lash out and run. "Well, I'm asking now."

He walked out to the porch and she followed. Leaning close, he pointed to the horizon, where the edge of the land folded down into a twisting canyon. "There," he said.

His face was so close to hers it made her heart beat faster. "What is it?"

"The perfect place for people to cross this section of the country unnoticed. They can travel for miles without being seen from the air or any lookout points."

Her spine tingled. "What kind of people?"

"Drug runners."

Like Feria. She tried to move away from him but the porch was too small. "What's Leeman's interest?"

"His property adjoins mine. If he ran me off and bought my land, he'd control the entire stretch of this valley. Anyone who wants to cross without a problem would grease his palm and off they'd go."

She saw the setting sun reflected in his eyes and thought about the strange lights she'd seen coming from the canyon. "What about you? Does anyone grease your palm?"

He laughed and held up his hands. "Does it look like it to you?"

"But Feria said you two were partners."

Booker stepped nearer to her, closing the gap between them. "Feria says a lot of things."

"He's a drug dealer."

"I know."

His face was inches from hers. She could see the worry and the pride, too, and something else that burned deep down in his eyes. Slowly he lowered his hands until he cupped her face.

"Things are always so much more complicated than they seem."

He leaned toward her. She held her breath, heart pounding, feet unable to move. She knew she should push him away, but she could not. A warmth seemed to wrap her up from the inside out. He pressed his stubbled cheek to hers and moved his lips down her neck until the found the place where her pulse hammered violently. After an endless moment, he sighed and let her go. "I'd better walk you to the cabin."

On shaking legs, she followed.

When he was gone she willed herself to relax. With Ace at her heels, she padded to the kitchen, found a packet of tea and steeped some for herself. In spite of the calming brew, she felt taut as a wire inside. What was she doing, letting Booker get that close to her? And enjoying the feel of his cheek next to hers? Had she learned nothing?

A memory swam into her head before she could screen it

out. She hadn't wanted to go to the party, but Jack had insisted. He pressed a drink into her hand and teased her until she brought it to her lips.

Moments later she began to feel strange, and her thinking became fuzzy. Jack helped her upstairs so she could lie down. She realized somewhere in the back of her mind that most of the partygoers were strangers to her—a few college students and many people she'd never seen before. One face she did recognize: a girl named Sue who had tried to befriend her when she arrived at college. She'd brushed the girl off and didn't even know her last name.

Feeling worse and worse, she was led to a bedroom to lie down. Head spinning, stomach spasming, she was hardly aware when Jack came in and started to undress her. She wanted to run, wanted to scream, but her body felt as if she'd been given a giant dose of Novocain.

Then Sue was there, somehow, berating Jack as he towered over her small frame.

"Get out, Sue. This isn't your business," Jack said.

"Maybe not, but I saw you put something into her drink. I'm not going to let you rape her."

"It isn't rape. She's my girlfriend."

"If she didn't say yes, it's rape. Now get out before I call the cops."

It was Sue who'd summoned a cab and escorted Anita back to her dorm room, insisting that she call the police.

Anita hadn't, out of fear and shame and the desire to make the whole awful thing disappear. "Why did you do that for me?" Anita had asked through her tears.

Sue smiled. "You didn't have anyone there to protect you, so I did."

As Anita stared out into the night, she wished Sue was there to protect her from the odd kaleidoscope of feelings that coursed through her now. Should she trust Booker? A man who had connections to Feria? A man on the edge of desperation?

She remembered the feeling of comfort his touch brought, the look of compassion in his eyes.

No, Anita.

Trust had almost gotten her raped, and she could no longer trust herself where people were concerned.

She couldn't allow herself to get in deeper with Booker.

The blackness outside mirrored her own feelings of despair. She was about to go to bed when the idea hit her like a slap.

Her brother needed her and he couldn't survive on his own much longer.

There was one person who knew the desert inside and out, only one person who could tell her where her brother was.

If only he didn't kill her first.

Booker made sure Anita got safely to the cabin. Ace trotted in after her, which eased Booker's mind. The closer they edged to her brother, the worse things seemed to get. He had an irrational feeling that someone was watching them, waiting for the chance to go after Anita for some unknown reason. Why?

If Anita was right, someone had been looking to frame Drew, but something had gone wrong. The stolen camera proved that. A sinister thought entered his mind. Leeman had seemed pretty broken up by his wife's death, but what if it was an act? Robin said Heidi was scared of her husband. Maybe she was right to be frightened of him. If Heidi had something incriminating on Cyrus, he'd get it back one way or another, Booker knew. A picture of Heidi's body rose in his mind.

His suspicions were unsettling, but what scared him more at the moment was his reaction to Anita on the porch. He had every reason to despise her, but what he felt was nothing close to that emotion. His lips still tingled from the feel of her neck, the silk of her skin smooth on his fingers. He wanted to lock her in an embrace and ease all the worry from her mind, to protect her; a woman whom he knew was perfectly capable of taking care of herself.

He opened the dresser drawer and took out the velvet box. The cabochon inside seemed to glow with its own luminescence. Moving it closer to the lamplight, he could see the iridescent blue and green play across the surface. A spark of red fire twinkled there, too. It was a gorgeous opal, and he could probably get five hundred for it, definitely enough to get the utility company off his back.

With a sigh, he put it back in the drawer, kicking himself for the foolish sentimentality that he could not understand. He checked the answering machine again. No potential tour customers. Reluctantly, he booted up the computer and perused the e-mails. No encouraging messages there, either. With a sense of dread, he looked at his bank account balance. Thanks to the payment from the tour, he could cover the electricity, but it would leave very little left over for windmill repairs.

No windmill, no water.

No water meant dead cattle—not that there were many left, anyway, but one small herd would bring in enough at auction to repair the roof and buy a used truck. It would keep them going—for a while, anyway.

He sighed. Maybe the mill would hold up just a little longer. With his luck, he doubted it.

Restlessness drove him to the window. He looked out across the dark ground.

It whispered across his mind again. There was a way to save his land. All he had to do was put out his hand and look the other way.

Feria knew Booker was desperate.

He knew Booker would do anything to save his ranch.

Anything.

Lord, help me hold on.

The next morning, after Booker returned from checking the fence line and dropping a half-dozen bales of hay to supplement the herd's meager grazing, Sergeant Williams called and requested they come to the station to answer more questions. Anita nodded when he told her, toying with a slice of toast more than eating it.

She looked pale, nervous.

"Comfortable in the cabin?"

"Yes." She put down the toast and sipped some coffee. "Ace stayed right by my side all night."

"Mmmm. He's better than a shadow."

She nodded. "While we're in town, I've got to run an errand. Do you mind?"

Though he wondered what it might be, he kept the question to himself. "No problem. I've got to go pay the electric bill and schedule with the farrier to reshoe my horse." *Hope he'll take credit this time.*

Was it his imagination or was there a look of resolution in Anita's eyes, as if she'd decided to go down a path he wasn't privy to? He could press, but he had a feeling she'd clam up. He was rescued from an awkward silence by the phone. After hanging up, he explained to Anita.

"Guy across town needs some help running fence line. One of his help is sick so he needs a fill-in." He hesitated. "Didn't get any tour jobs today, so it would help to bring in a couple bucks."

She gave him a smile. "Of course. One tour complete with rattlesnakes is enough for a few days."

He chuckled. "Yeah. You going to be okay? I can drive you back here after your errand. Or if there's someplace else you'd rather go."

"No need. Just take me to the police station, then I'll do my errands and go to the library. I want to do some research on *Wild World Magazine.* You can pick me up when you're done."

He felt a sliver of unease. "You sure?"

"Absolutely. I've thrown off your schedule enough, Booker. Please do what you need to do."

Reluctantly, he agreed. "Let's go get this police business over with."

"I'm with you."

They drove under heavily clouded skies to the police station. Booker could not shake the strange feeling of foreboding as they entered.

Sergeant Williams ushered them into the conference room and turned to Anita. "How are you holding up?"

"About as well as you can when your brother is missing and people are trying to frame him for murder."

Her face remained impassive. "We're still trying to piece together the whole business. There's no trace of Diego, so we can't confirm his story."

Booker cleared his throat. "If it means anything, Diego's a good guy, just trying to survive and all that. He didn't have to help us."

"We'll keep looking for him, anyway. It's possible he had something to do with Heidi Leeman's death."

Anita frowned. "That doesn't make sense that he'd lead us back to the crime scene."

"He didn't. He led you to the place where Drew was hiding and you found a clue that sent you to the tower. It's possible Diego wanted you to follow it, wanted you to find the body, to further incriminate your brother."

"Seems far-fetched." Booker folded his arms across his wide chest. "Lot of trouble to go through for nothing."

Anita nodded. "What would he gain?"

The officer leveled a look at them. "Outwardly, nothing, but maybe he was paid by someone."

Anita straightened. "Paid? By whom?"

She shrugged. "Don't know. Someone who has an interest in seeing your brother go down. Know anyone who might fit that bill?"

"Leeman," Anita said.

Williams nodded. "I thought you would say that, but why? What reason would he have to frame your brother?"

"Because he killed his wife and needs someone else to take the fall."

The lack of surprise on Williams's face made Booker realize she had mulled over that possibility, too.

"Did you find out how Heidi Leeman died?" Booker asked her.

"Yes. Gunshot."

Anita shuddered.

Booker shook his head. The poor woman. According to Robin, she'd lived in fear and now it seemed she'd died that way, too. "Did Robin Hernando tell you that Heidi was afraid of her husband? She wanted to leave him."

"Yes, she told me. She also told me that Drew came to meet her at the ranch a few times and they spoke on the phone on at least one occasion. Gershwin confirms that he observed Drew in close conversation with Mrs. Leeman many times at the *Wild World* office."

Anita stared blankly. "He was being kind, trying to help her out."

"Maybe."

"Maybe? What other explanation is there?"

"They were involved. They met for a rendezvous. Lovers' spat ensued. Drew killed her."

"No. I won't believe that."

Booker cupped a hand over Anita's shoulder. "That's just a theory. One of many the police are looking at, I'm sure."

Williams tapped her pencil on the table. "It's the one that fits the best with the crime scene evidence, unfortunately. We interviewed Robin and her staff. A couple of days ago her head guy, Carlos, saw Drew leaving from the direction of the overlook on his motorcycle in a real hurry about the time we suspect the woman was killed."

"Did Carlos see any other vehicles leaving?"

She shook her head. "It was just before nightfall, and he'd

left the area to attend business at the house. It's possible another vehicle was present and he didn't see it."

"Possible?" There was an edge to Anita's voice. "But you don't think so."

Williams sighed. "In my business, Ms. Teel, you get a few cases that are real stumpers, but most of them are what they seem to be—acts of temper, greed, desperation."

Anita stiffened. "Did you find my brother's fingerprints on the murder weapon?"

"No."

He heard Anita's breath come out in a rush before she answered. "There, you see? That proves he didn't kill her."

"Not exactly. There were no prints at all on the gun. It had been wiped clean. Nevertheless—" she pulled a gun in a heavy plastic bag out of a drawer and dropped it on the desktop "—this gun, the one that killed Heidi, was purchased by your brother a week ago at a local gun shop."

Anita put her hands on the officer's desk. "That is not possible. He's never owned a gun."

Booker remembered their search of Drew's ravaged apartment. He remembered, too, the look on Anita's face when he pointed out the box of Techshot Pistol Cartridges to her. Drew may have hated guns, but the fact was that he'd purchased bullets, anyway, and now, it appeared, a weapon, too. Though Anita didn't want to believe it, the truth could not be ignored. The ugly hardware used to brutally stamp out a life was her brother's.

"What can I do?" Her words came out in a whisper. "Is there anything I can say to help you see he didn't do this awful thing?"

Williams fixed her with a look that was not altogether unkind. "Find him and pray he's got a real good explanation."

Anita followed numbly as Booker took her with great reluctance to the library's quiet study room where she could hook up her laptop.

"I don't feel right about leaving you," he said, brow furrowed.

"Go. I'll be fine. I'm just going to do some research, after I pray."

He slid onto the chair across from her and grabbed her hand. "Father God, please watch over Drew and give us all the strength and courage to find our way to the truth. Amen."

She felt tears dangerously close to the surface. "Thank you. I haven't prayed with anyone since my parents died."

He flushed slightly and let go of her hand after a final squeeze. "No problem. God's used to hearing from me. Practically got Him on speed dial."

She watched him go, his tall frame filling the doorway. Again, a strange longing took over inside. How could he be that good to her? After everything? And why did she feel like she could get through anything as long as he was by her side?

She shook herself. *No. There is no room in your life for another romantic disaster. You will find your brother by yourself the next time you have the opportunity.* The thought of Feria's knife pressed to her throat made her shiver.

FIFTEEN

Anita lost herself in research until she looked up and checked the clock. Still another hour until the electronics store opened. With resolution, she returned her attention to her laptop and resumed the comforting exercise of researching, a skill learned by long hours acquiring information on her bats.

She caught a glimpse of the many folders filled with painstakingly acquired data from her trip to the Seychelles. How excited she'd been only days ago, seeing that beautiful wave of sheath-tailed bats stream out against the darkening sky. She hoped she'd have the chance to return, to finish her critical research before the bats were crowded out by human activity or smothered by the voracious kudzu vine that would eventually weave itself into an impenetrable tapestry across the cave mouth. The work that was the core of her life seemed as far away as her brother.

She sighed and clicked open an Internet connection, typing *Wild World Magazine* into the search engine. "All right, Mr. Leeman. Let's see if I can find out what you're hiding."

The screen brought up the magazine's Web site, which showed snippets from the latest issue. She learned only that the magazine had been started ten years earlier by Cyrus Leeman, who had previously been editor in chief of several smaller periodicals.

She refined the search terms and began to focus in on the owner himself. Many hits revealed that Leeman was often quoted in articles as "the successful entrepreneurial model." Facts about his personal life were scant. There was a reference to Leeman's father, who owned several hotels and a football team before he died in his late sixties. No tidbits about his mother. Anita found several places where Heidi was mentioned as a member of certain social and charitable organizations concerned with adult literacy and animal rights.

She was about to delve deeper when the door to the small room opened and Paul Gershwin came in, looking haggard.

"Sorry to barge in. Is it okay?" He stood uncertainly, holding a backpack in one hand.

Anita gestured to a chair across from her. "Please sit."

"Thanks. I was returning some books and I saw you back here."

She watched him flop down and prop his elbows on the table. "Are you okay? You look tired."

His laugh was humorless. "I'm running around sticking my fingers in the leaks, but the dam is breaking apart anyway. I was able to scramble and cover the missing stories Drew was going to handle, but now that Heidi…" He shook his head. "The boss hasn't really been able to do much important decision making in view of what's happened."

"I'm sorry, Paul, really sorry about Heidi, but my brother didn't kill her. You know that, right?"

He looked at the tabletop. "I want to believe it, but the evidence seems to be piling up. And Leeman, well, I'm afraid if your brother does show his face again, Leeman will kill him on sight, guilty or not."

Remembering the look of rage on Leeman's face when he'd thrown himself on Booker, Anita did not doubt it for a moment. "You know Leeman better than anyone. How long have you worked at *Wild World?*"

Paul considered. "Almost nine years. I came in just after he got the magazine going. It was a great opportunity to help shape the direction of the company, or so I thought. Turns out

Leeman did the shaping, and my opinions weren't needed. He made that clear to me from the beginning."

"What do you think of him?"

Paul raised an eyebrow. "He's a shrewd businessman, intelligent, made a success out of the magazine in a climate where most periodicals are going the way of the dinosaur. It's an extremely difficult thing to put out a magazine. You've got to know the business and you've got to know the marketing end, too. He's been fair to me in terms of pay, I guess. Of course, I'd like more responsibility after nine years of proving myself."

"How did he treat Heidi?"

Paul seemed startled by the question. "Frankly, I never understood what she saw in him, other than his success, of course. He was condescending to her, patronizing at times. I would have felt sorry for her but Heidi didn't seem to let it get her down. She always had a smile, an encouraging word for everyone."

"Did you think she was afraid of Leeman?"

"Afraid? Probably, just like we all are to some degree. I noticed she hung around the office a lot more when he was away traveling, but everyone was more relaxed when he was gone."

"Did she spend much time with my brother?"

He shifted. "Maybe. It's a friendly office. We all went out to lunch and things like that. Drew did seem to hit it off with Heidi, but most men did. She is, was, a very charming woman."

Anita tried to think of what to ask next to shed light on the whole mess.

Paul eyed her. "Things aren't looking up for your brother, are they? I heard about the gun."

She nodded. "I think it was planted."

He toyed with the strap of his backpack but didn't answer.

"Paul? Do you know something you're not telling me?"

He pushed the glasses farther up on his nose. "I'm not sure what to say anymore. I'm stuck in the middle of my friendship with Drew and my loyalty to Leeman and Heidi."

"What is it? You've got to tell me."

"I don't know."

She reached out a hand and clasped his forearm. "Please, Paul. I'm running out of time."

He heaved a sigh. "Leeman said there are accounting records erased from the computer. Well, one night I came by the office late, and your brother was there. He shoved something, which I thought was a disk, into his pack and made some excuse about working on photo editing before he took off."

"What do you think was really going on?"

"I'm not sure, but I think he was on the office computer when he had no reason to be, the main computer where Heidi and our other bookkeeper did most of the accounting stuff."

"Are you certain?"

"Pretty much. I went over and felt the read/write unit and it was still warm."

"So he was burning a disk? Why?"

Paul shrugged. "I forgot about it until this whole thing came up. I wonder…well, I suspect, maybe…"

"What?"

"That he was covering his tracks somehow, that maybe he was stealing money like Leeman said. I can't think of any other reason he'd need to be on that computer."

She sank lower in the chair with a groan.

"I'm sorry. I didn't bring up this info to the police because I wasn't sure. It was just a feeling on my part that something wasn't quite right. I hate to add anything to the pile that makes it harder for you and Drew."

"One thing that doesn't make sense, though. If Drew did do all these things, why would someone need to work so hard to keep me away from the truth?"

"How do you mean?"

"First my tires were punctured when I got to Rockridge. Then someone tossed his apartment looking for something, his camera was stolen and we were nearly driven off the road.

Whoever it was thinks Drew has given me something that would incriminate him or her."

"Has he? Given you anything, I mean?"

She pressed her hands together. "No. That's just it. I got the one phone call and then nothing. There's nothing in his apartment, no messages except the one about the overlook at Robin's."

"How did he communicate that location to you? Maybe there's something else there you missed."

"I don't think so. Whatever we didn't see, the police would have found."

"What about the man? I heard a Mexican guy led you there. Is it possible he removed something?"

Anita frowned. "I never thought of that. I suppose anything is possible. Someone is desperate enough to attack Booker for the camera, so I shouldn't rule anyone out. I can't believe it's Diego, though."

"Who do you think it is?"

She didn't speak, but he must have seen the answer written on her face.

"Leeman? What would he gain from it? Seems like he wants Drew found and punished."

"Unless Drew knows something that would incriminate him."

Paul's eyes widened. "This is all a muddle to me. I'm a great editor, but not much of a detective."

She gave him a smile. "You and me both."

"I should have followed my instincts and become a sailor. Investigation is not for me."

"I guess that's why we rely on the police for these kinds of things." A thought occurred to her. "Paul, what do you think about Agent Rogelio?"

Paul raised an eyebrow. "Him? Why? Is he putting the moves on you?"

She colored. "Not exactly." *I haven't given him the chance.* "I just wondered if he's trustworthy."

"Leeman seems to think so. They spend a lot of time together. Rogelio was always happy to stop in and talk to Heidi, too. A real ladies' man. Can't think what the girls see in him, but he's been married three times so there must be something." He fiddled with his glasses. "If you think of anything I can help with, let me know. Heidi really was a wonderful woman and, however it turns out, she deserves justice."

Anita watched him go. Justice? Would there be any for her brother?

She worked on the computer for a while longer without success, even pulling up Agent Rogelio's name. All she got was a screen full of nothing. When her eyes began to burn, she closed the laptop and headed into the hot, gray afternoon to the electronics store.

The man stocking shelves looked down from his perch on the stepladder and eyed her with curiosity. "Help you?"

"I need a satellite phone."

His eyes widened. "Sure about that? We get cell coverage in most places here. The SAT phones are expensive."

Anita tried to keep her voice even. "Yes, I know. I have plenty of experience with SAT phones. Do you have them or not?"

He climbed down from the ladder and led her to a display. "Only got one kind."

"Fine. That will do."

"They're bulky, see, and not many people go for them unless they travel to remote locations."

Where this one was going, was plenty remote. "I'll take it."

He slid the box from the shelf. "Gonna cost you about a thousand dollars and change."

She swallowed. There went a good chunk of her savings. "No problem." She slid her own satellite phone out of her purse. "Can you help me program my phone number into that one?"

He gasped. "But you already got yourself a fancy phone. What you need another one for?"

This time her impatience got the better of her. "Trust me, I need it. Now please, can you program my number in the new phone or not?"

He shrugged and worked on the unit. "Here you go."

She stayed in the store long enough to test it, to make sure that one push of a button would connect the new phone to hers. She paid the curious clerk and left with the heavy phone stashed in her bag.

The combination of two bulky SAT phones and her laptop weighed her down as she stepped into the noon heat. Sweat beaded on her forehead. It was still several hours, she figured, before Booker was likely to be finished with his fence mending. She decided to head for the little coffee shop across the street to find some lunch. Ignoring the stares from curious patrons, Anita ordered a tuna on rye and sat down to munch her sandwich and guzzle a cool diet soda.

She was lingering there, enjoying the air-conditioning, when she saw Rogelio's SUV pull up outside the police station.

Heart quickening, she decided on a plan. Dialing Booker's cell number, she was relieved to get his voice mail. She left a message and waited patiently, watching through the window until Rogelio came out. Then she shouldered her bag and walked in his direction, wielding the bulky load with a little more difficulty than was necessary. As she walked abreast of his car, he got out.

"Hey there, Ms. Teel. That's quite a full bag you're carrying. Can I give you a lift somewhere?"

She gave him a winning smile. "Oh, would you? I'm staying in the guest cabin on Booker's property. I'd sure appreciate a ride back there."

"I'd be happy to." He gallantly stowed her gear in the back-seat and opened the door for her. "May I buy you a soda first?"

"No, thank you. I just had one."

He looked disappointed. "Oh, I see. Lunch, then?"

"I had that, too, I'm afraid."

"Just my luck. I guess I'll be eating peanut butter and jelly at my desk again."

She ignored his pitiful tone. "Are you sure it isn't too much trouble? Giving me a lift, I mean?"

"Not at all. I could drive there and back blindfolded." He started up the engine and pulled away from the curb.

"Do you patrol that area a lot?"

He nodded. "Seems that way. Leeman and Scott are close enough to the border to have issues that need my attention." He puffed up a bit as he spoke. "Illegals, drug runners, that kind of thing."

"Can't you stop it?"

"Sure we could, with enough manpower—" he shot her a look "—and cooperation from the property owners."

"They don't cooperate with you? I can't believe it."

He laughed. "You know Booker Scott and you can't believe it? As stubborn a man as anyone I've ever met, including his father."

"So you've been in Rockridge a long time?"

"Yes, ma'am." He eyed a flash in the sky. "Looks like another dry storm. Not good after so many years of drought. Not good at all."

She tried to keep the conversation going. "This is a nice town."

"It has its good points. I've got my eye on other places, though, places with cool breezes and lots of green, where everything isn't completely parched."

"Sounds nice. Where?"

"Hawaii, maybe. Palm Springs. I'm looking to retire in a few years."

"Retire? You look young for that." She could see he was pleased by the remark.

"It's a dangerous job, wears you down after a while, and the money isn't worth getting a bullet in your back. I'm interested in buying a nice condo somewhere and living the quiet life." He looked over at her. "What about you? You looking to stay in Rockridge? Maybe with Booker?"

She felt her cheeks flame. "Me? No. Definitely not." The

idea of staying in Rockridge was not distasteful; she was be-ginning to feel at home in the rugged town with its austere cliffs and spectacular landscape. Making a life with Booker? The thought danced in her mind until she shook it away. *Just a little longer, Anita, until you get your brother back.*

Realizing Rogelio was waiting for her to say more, she blurted, "I've got a lot of research to do still, plenty of places to travel."

"Good plan. Tying yourself down here with Booker Scott would be plain stupid."

"Can I ask why?"

Rogelio shrugged. "He's a cow jockey, small-time rancher on a hunk of land he's going to lose anyway. He'll wind up a mechanic in some greasy garage working for a few bucks an hour."

The words sparked anger in her gut but she maintained control. "Why are you so sure he'll lose his land?"

"Just a theory."

"I don't think so. Leeman wants him off that land and you're pretty close to Leeman. Are you pressuring him, too?"

An expressionless mask seemed to slip over the agent's face. "What Leeman wants is his business."

"But he's pretty persuasive."

"And clever. Got you to carry the banner to the town council and shut down Booker's mine so he didn't even have to get his hands dirty."

Anita stiffened. It was true; she couldn't deny it. College-educated, top-of-her-class Anita Teel was used by a man again and, again, she hadn't seen it coming. As they drove up to the ranch house, Anita couldn't keep her eyes from the direction of the mine. At least the bats were safe, she consoled herself.

Bits of a long-ago conversation flitted in her mind.

"I can take precautions. The pocket I want to work is a mile away from the cave mouth. I can widen the vent that runs in from the side and mine without disturbing their roost. At least let me work out a plan."

She heard her own voice, cold and unyielding. "They have a small number of maternity roosts, and each one is critical due to loss of habitat to mining and agave harvests in Mexico."

Booker's face had been a mixture of surprise and disbelief. "I'm telling you I've lived on this ranch all my life. The bats are important to me, too, for insect control and just because when they come out at night it's like a wind that sweeps over this place. But Anita, you and I both know these bats migrate farther south into Mexico during the winter. Let me work my land, with proper care, when they're not here. We're talking a one-man show here, not a commercial mining setup."

She'd seen it in his face. He was not just asking because of his land. He'd needed her to believe in him, to trust him.

"I'm sorry." But she hadn't been sorry, not until later when she'd realized the real reason she'd lashed out at him and run. The real reason was buried in the memory of that dark room with Jack.

Rogelio parked the car in the driveway, opened the door for her and retrieved her bag from the trunk. He walked her to the door of the cabin. Her pulse quickened. Would he try to come in? She wished Booker hadn't taken Ace along with him.

He pushed his hat back with his thumb. "If you're going to be in town awhile, how about I take you to dinner one night?"

She thought frantically. "I'm not the best company, these days. Too worried about my brother. As soon as we find him, I'm going to leave."

His black eyes were unreadable as he looked at her. "You sure that's the reason you don't want to go out with me?"

She jerked. "Well, of course. What other reason could there be?"

He laid a hand on her shoulder, the fingers grazing the skin of her cheek. "Remember what I said about Booker. There's no future there."

She was paralyzed, praying he would leave. "I'll remember."

"Good." He moved his hand away and smiled. "I'll check back with you soon, see if you changed your mind about having dinner."

She felt a rush of relief as she closed the door firmly behind her. The feeling lasted only as long as it took her to peek out the front window. Rogelio was gone but the outline of a man standing in Booker's kitchen window started her pulse hammering again. The man was definitely not Booker.

SIXTEEN

Booker was hot and tired when he finished the fencing project in the late afternoon. His mood did not improve when he checked his messages and found out Anita had gotten a ride from Rogelio. Did she know what kind of a man he was? Did she care?

He poured water into a paper cup and let Ace drink his fill before they drove back to the ranch. As the miles went by, his mind raced. Rogelio was tight with Leeman, the very reason why he struggled with trusting the man. Could he trust him now?

Not completely, he had to admit to himself. Something about Heidi Leeman's murder gnawed away at him. If Leeman had killed his wife, maybe he'd enlisted Rogelio's help in covering it up and framing Drew. And Anita was happy to jump in the guy's car. He ground his teeth together. Ace put his head on Booker's knee.

"I know you like her, Ace, but she can drive a man crazy, you know that?"

The dog responded by giving Booker a lick on the wrist.

She was probably safe in the cabin, nose stuck in her computer, he told himself. The thought of seeing her there, waiting for him, lifted his mood. It was only temporary, he reminded himself. They'd certainly not let any love grow between them. Strictly a partnership to find her brother.

He felt the dog's gaze, staring at Booker's face as though he could look right into his heart. "Awww, come on, Ace. Don't let her fool you. She needs our help, that's all. Nothing more. She'll be out of here the first chance she gets."

He rolled down the window. A bank of dark clouds hung over the horizon, though the day was hot and still. A fork of light shot down from the clouds for a split second before it vanished.

More rain was what they needed, not the empty promise of distant clouds. The last few storms had only succeeded in soaking the desiccated topsoil. He pressed the accelerator harder and covered the miles quickly.

Ace became aware that something was up before he did. As soon as they pulled onto the long graveled driveway, the dog sat straight, back rigid, big ears swiveling around like radar dishes.

"What it is, boy?" Booker scanned in every direction but saw nothing amiss. The guest cabin was quiet, curtains drawn. He pushed the Jeep a little faster, and they arrived at the door in a shower of dust. Breaking into a jog, he found the front door unlocked. Ace jumped on stiff legs, clawing at the door until Booker opened it.

The dog shot inside and began to bark.

Booker ran after him until he got to the living room, where he stopped in shock.

An elderly man sat in the high-backed rocker, patting the now-ecstatic dog. "Hello, son."

Anita sat across from them, a smile brightening her face, eyes aglow.

Booker laughed out loud and crossed the room quickly to hug his father. "Hello, Pops. I'm glad to see you. How did you get here?"

The man's eyes sparkled in his wrinkled face. Booker looked for signs of weariness and found none. He was glad to note his father had put on a few pounds, and his frame was not as gaunt as it had been in the months following the stroke. Just the sight of him sitting there in the ranch that he'd worked so hard to build erased some of Booker's fatigue.

"Heard there's been some trouble around here so I came to

check things out. A fellow who was making deliveries at the apartments gave me a lift." He eyed Booker closely. "You look like you've been doing an honest day's work."

Booker sank down on the sofa. "Yes, sir. Mending fences on the Richards' property."

Pops looked thoughtful. "No tours today, I see."

He hated to admit it to his father. "No, sir. Business has been slow." He looked at Anita. "Anita helped me out on the last one. Have you two been catching up?"

Anita laughed. "Only for a few minutes before you got here. I thought he was a burglar at first."

The elder Scott laughed. "She came over wielding a rake. Good thing I saw her coming or I'd have been flattened."

Booker joined in the laughter. "She's a determined lady, all right." He spied his father's suitcase in the hallway. "Are you staying for a visit, Pops?"

"For as long as I'm needed."

The comment worried Booker. It had taken both their strength to decide the ranch life was too much for Dad. Moving him back home, as much as Booker cherished the idea, might be the death of him in his still-frail condition.

Anita seemed to pick up on the look that passed between them. She stood. "I'm going to cook supper for you menfolk tonight."

"You don't need to do that." Booker half rose. "I'll fix up something."

She held up a hand. "I insist. You've done nothing but feed me and shuttle me around the past few days. I'll cook while you two catch up and I won't hear any arguments about it."

Booker grinned. "Like I said, a determined lady."

When they were alone, Booker moved to the chair next to his father. "This ranch isn't the same without you."

He nodded. "Down to a hundred head, I noticed."

Booker sighed. "Had to sell them off."

"Figured you would. Roof still needs fixing and the south-end windmill."

He gritted his teeth. He'd hoped against all odds that he could pull off a miracle for his father to come back to, but he'd failed. The place was closer to the brink of bankruptcy than ever. "Hard times."

They sat in silence for a moment before his father spoke. "You've done your best, son. I want to come back and help."

"I really appreciate that, Pops, but—"

"I know I can't ride or herd, but I can answer phones, maybe even fix fences, and I can still throw a stew together."

"Pops, there's nothing I want more than for you to come home, but I'm scared about your health."

The old man fixed sharp blue eyes on him. "You're struggling. This ranch is struggling. My place is here. I've done enough convalescing, and I'm sure I can come back without being a burden."

"It's not a matter of being a burden. I don't want you to hurt yourself."

"You let me worry about that." He stretched his arms over his head. "I'm going to take a walk."

"I'll go with you."

"No, you go on in the kitchen and see if you can help that little lady." He winked at Booker. "How often do we have a woman come and volunteer to cook for us?"

"Pops, she's—"

He waved a hand. "I don't need to know any more right now. I'm just going to go watch the sunset. Got to get joy where you can when you're my age, and sunsets are still free, aren't they?" He walked slowly out the door and down the steps.

Ace stood, tail wagging, a question in his canine eyes as he turned his head to look first at Booker and then at Pops.

"Watch Pops," Booker said, and Ace trotted happily outside.

He felt a mixture of fear and joy as he took the suitcase to the big bedroom that had remained empty since his father's stroke. To have him here, back on the ranch, was the best thing, wasn't it?

Deep in thought, he made his way to the kitchen and found Anita, cheeks pink, hovering over a steaming pot.

"I hope spaghetti and meatballs are okay. I found some ground beef in the fridge and I figured it was the best course of action."

He smiled. "The steam makes your hair curlier."

"Good for the skin, too. Instant facial."

"If you say so." He took out the silverware and began to set the table.

"Where's your father?"

"Out for a walk."

She stirred the simmering pot. "Are you happy that he's home?"

"I've prayed for him to come home every day since his stroke."

She wiped her hands on a towel. "Then why do you look so worried?"

He sighed. "Because my father is a stubborn man who thinks he can accomplish anything through hard work and won't quit even when he should."

He was surprised to hear her laugh. "Sounds like you come by it honestly."

He stared for a moment before he laughed, too. "I guess you're right. I'm just afraid he'll hurt himself, or worse."

She walked over and gave Booker a hug.

He wrapped his arms around her, relishing the feel of her head tucked under his chin until she pulled away.

"I'll do whatever I can to help until…" she murmured.

"Until you have to leave."

She nodded.

Why did the thought of her departure make his gut clench? He closed his eyes for a moment. How had his life gotten so complicated in the few days since she'd arrived?

His thoughts were cut short as Anita began to put food on the table.

Before he went to get his father for dinner, he took one more look at Anita, humming as she bustled around the table.

* * *

Anita was pleased with her culinary efforts. The process of making dinner took her mind off her brother's dire situation. *You can't do anything about that now.* She thought of the SAT phone stowed safely in the cabin. *Not yet, anyway.*

Instead she piled the spaghetti and meatballs on a platter and sliced the garlic bread. There had been no greens for a salad, so she went with frozen peas instead. Pops and Booker sat down at the table.

"Heavenly Father," Pops began. "Bless this meal and these fine people seated here. For this night, for this blessing of food, we give You our must humble thanks. Amen."

The table broke into cheerful conversation as Pops regaled them with stories. The expression on Booker's face was so tender it broke her heart. She fervently hoped Pops had made the right decision to come home, for both their sakes.

After all three of them cleaned up the table and dishes, Booker disappeared into the night to check the windmill, leaving Pops and Anita sitting on the porch in search of a cool evening breeze. It was fruitless, as the temperature seemed even hotter than the previous day. The air hung hot and stifling around them.

Moonlight, filtered through the thick layer of fog, dotted the landscape with pools of silver. Pops sighed. "Oh, I've missed this place, that's for sure."

She looked out toward the horizon, eyes instinctively drawn to the cave, though it was too far away to see. "Mr. Scott, I...I need to talk to you about something."

"Only if you call me Pops. Mr. Scott sounds like someone from *Star Trek.*"

She laughed. "Okay, if you'll call me Anita. I wanted to tell you, to say, that I'm sorry for causing you trouble on my last visit here."

He cocked his head. "About the mine?"

"Yes. I thought I was doing the right thing, to save the bats, but it turned out to be more complicated than I realized. I didn't take the time to see the whole picture, and I let other people influence me. I'm sorry. I'm truly sorry."

He nodded. "I know that. I can hear it in your voice."

"I just feel so terrible. I know that the ranch is struggling. Booker's been working so hard."

"Being able to mine the opals wouldn't have magically erased all our troubles."

"No, but it would have helped."

He rocked the old chair. "What's done is done. Only one thing I'd like to know."

"What?"

"How come you didn't tell Booker all this? Hurt him pretty bad, you dropping this on him and leaving. Felt like he'd read you all wrong."

Her heart thumped painfully. "I've tried to apologize, but I didn't really see things clearly until just recently."

"Anita, I've seen plenty in my day. I can call a spade a spade. I think you know the real reason. Why did you lash out and run?"

She closed her eyes at the question that she'd asked herself many times in the quiet of her soul. "Because I was afraid to stay."

He was quiet for a long while, the only sound from the squeak of the rocking chair. "Afraid to trust Booker?"

She managed a nod.

"Thing is, Anita, if you'll forgive an old man for saying so, it's not Booker you're afraid to trust, honey. It's yourself."

It was true and she knew it, but hearing it out loud was too much. Tears crowded her eyes and her throat thickened. They sat in silence for a while, staring out at the ranch land, each lost in their own thoughts. When she heard Booker and Ace returning, Anita got up, unwilling to face Booker in her present state.

She kissed Pops on the cheek and he patted her hand.

"We're glad the Lord brought you back here, Anita. You bring a happiness to Booker that he needs, whether or not he can admit it."

She headed through the darkness to the cabin. Happiness? She didn't bring happiness to anyone. She'd run away from Jack and then Booker, and pretty soon she'd fly from this place again. Pops was right. She didn't trust herself to give her heart to the right person, probably never would.

That left only one thing to do. Find Drew and run.

SEVENTEEN

Ace had settled on sleeping outside halfway between the cabin and ranch house. His barking woke Booker, who sat up with a jolt. For a moment he could not make sense of what had awakened him until the dog's frantic noises roused him completely. Through bleary eyes he checked the time—1:30 a.m. His first thought was Anita. Whoever was after Drew had gotten to her.

Hurling himself out of bed and into a pair of jeans and a T-shirt, he ran to the front door. Ace greeted him with hoarse barks.

"What is it?" He'd sprinted several yards toward the cabin when it filtered through his senses.

His father appeared at the door of the house. "Smoke."

"Yeah." A plume of black was funneling up in the distance against the moonlight, like an enormous cloud of bats. Booker returned to the house, grabbed the keys and raced to the Jeep. "Stay here, Pops."

"I'll go with you."

"I need you to check on Anita. Make sure she's okay." He gunned the engine and took off toward an orange glow in the distance, Ace in the seat next to him.

He flew down the road, ignoring the bouncing and jostling as the vehicle hit every uneven patch. All the while his heart raced. Fire. A rancher's worst nightmare. In this heat, even a small fire could wipe out hundreds of thousands of acres and nothing would slow it down, not even the few days of rain they'd had.

Just what we need. Lord, help us.

He crested the ridge and got a closer look. Down in a hollow, the windmill stood a hundred yards from a wood shed where they stored the tools and supplemental feed. The shed burned ferociously, sending out pops of flame.

For a moment, he was paralyzed by the sight of it. Then he slammed the Jeep in gear and headed for the water hookup at the base of the big tank.

He didn't feel the metal cut into his hands as he jammed the hose connector home and turned on the water. It was almost laughable. The low pressure delivered a steady stream that seemed to do nothing but anger the flames, which crackled and spewed from the shed. He tried to find the base of the blaze and concentrate the water stream there, but the fire had grown to engulf the little building. Fire poured out the window and shot through the place where the door had been.

Acrid smoke clouded around him as he desperately aimed the water.

He knew in his gut his efforts were useless, but his mind wouldn't sign on.

He continued to move as close as he dared, the heat baking his skin as if he'd stepped into a furnace. Sweat rolled down his face, stinging his eyes and trickling down his cheeks.

A truck raced up. Anita and Pops got out and hustled over.

"We called the fire department," Pops yelled over the noise of the fire. "They're fifteen minutes away."

In fifteen minutes, it won't be worth the gas it takes to get here. Because he didn't want to see the look in his father's eyes, or the pity on Anita's face, he directed them to move back and continued to face the fire until sirens echoed in the distance.

When the fire truck rolled up and the uniformed personnel jumped off the rig, he moved aside and watched as they unfurled hoses. Gallons of water rushed out, drowning the flames until the fire died away.

It was too little, too late. The shed was a smoking wreck, and all the tools and hay he'd stored there were destroyed. The firefighters continued to drench the mess, then switched to long metal tools and poked through the burned debris to be sure no hot spots remained.

Booker leaned on the Jeep and watched in despair. Ace sat at his booted feet.

When Pops went to talk to the fire captain, Anita perched on the bumper next to Booker. "Was there much of value in there?"

He closed his eyes. "Enough."

She took his hand and squeezed, not saying a word.

He was grateful for her touch, grateful that she didn't give him a bunch of cheerful platitudes. They sat together, holding hands, her shoulder pressed to his, and they watched the smoke drift off against the moonlight.

Pops returned, and Anita insisted he take her resting spot on the bumper.

The old man sighed. "Chief says it was dry lightning. Hit the windmill and traveled along the ground until it found some fuel. Shed didn't stand a chance."

Booker nodded.

Anita frowned. "I never heard of dry lightning."

Pops pointed to an electric sizzle in the sky that vanished as quickly as it started. "Temperature's gotten so hot the rain evaporates before it reaches the ground. Couple years back our neighbors lost their home to dry lightning. We're lucky it was only the shed."

"Lucky," Booker repeated dully.

They all lapsed into silence for a while, watching the firefighters busy at their work.

Booker finally roused himself. "I'm going to stay out here tonight, make sure there are no flare-ups. You two go on back."

Pops shook his head. "I'll stay with you."

"Nothing to be accomplished here. What's done is done. Go back and get some rest. Tomorrow we can see if there's anything left to salvage." Looking at the smoking black remains, he didn't think that was likely.

Pops and Anita left reluctantly as a Border Patrol vehicle pulled up. Booker folded his arms and kept his gaze straight ahead on the firefighters. It didn't help. Rogelio found him anyway.

"Your luck goes from bad to worse."

Booker didn't answer.

"Got a cause yet?"

"Chief thinks it's dry lightning."

"Makes sense." Rogelio frowned in thought. "Of course, could be something else."

Booker shot him a look. "What?"

"Come on, Scott. You can't be that naive. Someone wants you to make a deal. Maybe this little blaze was meant to encourage you along those lines?"

Anger flared inside him. The thought, the idea, that someone would set a fire to send him a message made his blood boil. "I won't be bullied."

"No, I'm sure of that." He looked over the smoking shed. "Still, you've got a whole lot more reasons now to cooperate with him, don't you?"

Booker wanted to punch the arrogant look off of Rogelio's face. Instead he forced himself to take a calming breath. "I'll manage."

Rogelio laughed. "I can see how well you're managing. Down to one herd, tour business not exactly packing them in. Must have had some gear in your shed by the look on your face."

"I don't need your advice on how to run my ranch."

"Maybe you do if you're too stubborn to see what's in front of your face. Cooperating would solve all your problems, wouldn't it? Pay off your debts. Get some help for your dad if he needs it. Why don't you think about it? No sense carrying the weight of the world on your shoulders when there's an easier way."

"And maybe you should stick to the crime fighting."

Rogelio's eyes glowed eerily in the darkness. "It's the end result that matters, Booker, not how you got there."

"Doesn't sound like cop talk to me."

He shrugged. "Things are different here."

No, Booker thought. They're no different than anywhere else. Choices had to be made and lived with. Would he be able to live with his own? "I've got to go talk to the chief."

"Sure. Give me a call when you can see things clearly."

Booker didn't look back.

Anita finally persuaded Pops to climb into the truck and turned on the heater. "You look cold." The old man looked worse than cold, she thought. His hand trembled slightly where it rested on his knee and his eyes were deeply shadowed. She imagined the stress of the situation would not help his recovery from the stroke.

"Are you okay?"

Pops gave her a smile. "Yes, I'm okay. Not used to this type of excitement anymore. Nothing much happens at an assisted-living complex. Best part of my day was Booker's visits, and he's been trying so hard to make the tour business go, he hasn't come by as much."

She nodded, keeping her eyes on the dark road.

"Can you help?"

The question startled her. "With what?"

"His tour business. You're pretty tech savvy, he tells me. With all that research and Web writing you've done, can you help him learn how to advertise and all that?"

"I... I'm not sure. I guess I could show him a few things..." she hesitated "...if he wanted to learn."

Pops laughed. "You got a point there. He's a proud man, like his stubborn coot of a father. Maybe he wouldn't like taking lessons."

Especially from me. "And I won't be here very long. Just until we find my brother."

Pops considered. "I've got a better idea. How about you teach me how to work with this Internet monster? Until you have to leave, I mean." He rubbed a hand over his face. "I'm not good for much, but I can sit and click a mouse if you show me."

She laughed. "Deal."

"Maybe you can give me a crash course."

"I'd be happy to." Her heart lurched, remembering how she and her father used to keep up a snappy, e-mail repartee. She missed him and her mother so much sometimes it hurt to breathe. If she could just find her brother, maybe the desperate feeling inside her would ease.

They made it to the house as another car pulled up. Robin and Paul Gershwin got out and hurried over.

Robin wore perfectly tailored jeans and a silk tank. She took one look at Pops and threw her arms around him. "Oh, Pops. I didn't know you were back home. How wonderful to see you. But what has happened? We heard the sirens."

Pops hugged her and patted her shoulders. He nodded to Paul. "How's the shoulder, young fella?"

Paul smiled. "Anyone who calls me young fella is all right in my book. The shoulder is healing okay." He gave Anita a nod. "I wish I could say I injured it doing something heroic, but tearing a rotator cuff cleaning out gutters isn't too racy. And you, Pops? How's that dragon of a physical therapist treating you?"

Pops shrugged and patted Anita on the shoulder. "We saw each other the other day at the PT office. No pain, no gain?"

Paul's smile was rueful. "I've got the pain part, still waiting for the gain."

Pops laughed. "You get hold of that *Queen* yet?"

"Nah." Paul must have seen the confusion on Anita's face. "The *Queen Bee* is a boat. I was helping Heidi buy it for her husband as a surprise."

Thinking about Heidi's battered body made Anita shiver. Had she tried to buy a present for the man to placate him until she could leave? Or was it a ruse to keep Paul from finding out her plans? Anita took Pops by the arm and detached Robin. "Let's go inside and we'll fill you in."

Soon they were all seated in the living room with cups of coffee. Anita filled a thermos to deliver to Booker as soon as she could.

Pops finished telling Robin and Paul about the fire. "They think the cause was dry lightning. Booker's standing watch until morning."

Robin shook her head. "It's one disaster after another. I feel like I'm living in a bad movie."

Paul glanced at his watch. "I didn't realize how late it was. We were trying to put our heads together, to plan some sort of memorial for Heidi." He sighed. "Mr. Leeman is so focused on finding Drew he can't work on anything else, so I suggested to Robin that we should deal with it. We've been looking through old photos to find material."

Robin laughed. "Paul has been through every inch of my house."

He chuckled. "Seems that way. We got to gabbing, I guess. Lost track of time until we heard the sirens." He looked at Anita. "Are you staying here on the ranch?"

"In the guest cabin." She ignored the speculative look that rose in Robin's eyes. "What is Leeman doing to find my brother?"

"He's torn apart the office, first of all. Gone through every file cabinet and drawer looking for something that might tell him where your brother is holed up. Last I saw he was scanning the yellow pages for a private detective."

Anita sighed. "Well, at least that's one thing we see eye to eye on. I want my brother found as soon as possible, too."

Paul gave her a sympathetic look. "Still no word from him?"

"No."

"Maybe he's fled the state."

"I don't see how. Diego said he was hurt. His bike is totaled and the police are watching the train stations and airport."

"If he did kill Heidi…" Robin began.

Anita cut her off. "He didn't."

Robin's dark eyes narrowed. "Well, he must be involved in some way or another or he would have come forward before. He might have snuck over the border into Mexico."

"He isn't guilty. He's scared."

She stared at Anita. "Of Leeman?"

"Yes, and the police. He doesn't trust them."

"I don't know what to believe anymore. All I know is someone killed my friend and she didn't deserve that. Whoever is responsible, I hope they pay for it." Robin got to her feet. "I must go talk to Booker, to see if he's okay."

Anita's stomach clenched. "He said he didn't want us to stay with him. He asked me to take Pops back home."

She pushed the curtain of dark hair over her shoulder. "Well, he didn't give *me* any orders, and even if he did, he knows I'd never follow them." She eyed the thermos of coffee on the counter and took it. "I'll bring this to him."

Anita opened her mouth to retort and then closed it. If Booker wanted Robin to stay with him, there was nothing Anita could do about it. *It's not your business, anyway. Booker is free to spend time with whomever he wants.*

Robin laid a manicured hand on Paul's shoulder. "Will you drive me over there?"

"Sure. I've got my camera in the trunk. Maybe there will be some coyote action along the way or something. Goodness knows we're going to need something to fill up the magazine. We can't run forty pages of white space."

Robin laughed and gave Pops another hug. "Why don't you get some rest? We'll see ourselves off the property later." She kissed him and followed Paul out the door.

Anita walked to the window. She watched the lovely woman slide gracefully onto the passenger seat. Paul closed the door for her and the car headed down the drive.

Would Booker be happy to see Robin? Pleased to have her

to share his thoughts with? She blinked away an unexpected rush of tears.

Pops was behind her. He reached out a hand and laid it gently on her shoulder. "Don't worry about Robin," he said. "Booker only has one young lady in his heart."

He moved slowly down the hall. She waited until she heard the sound of the door softly close.

Only one young lady in his heart.

The words thrilled her. Could Pops be right? Was it possible she hadn't destroyed all his feelings by her betrayal? Though she knew she wouldn't allow herself to have a future with Booker, the idea made her heart ache with a mixture of sweet and bitter as she trudged back to the cabin.

EIGHTEEN

Booker sat on a flat rock and watched the sun rising against the darkness. Ace lay at his feet, a welcome spot of warmth against the cold of the morning. He wished he could feel the rush of joy he usually experienced when the morning sun washed the horizon in muted colors. All he felt on this morning was fatigue and a sense of defeat.

Robin had offered help when she arrived the previous night. "Whatever you need to get you through." Her caress on his arm left no doubt that she was still hoping for a relationship with him. He puzzled over it. She was a beautiful woman, loyal and generous. Why didn't he feel anything for her? he wondered.

Because someone else lingered in his heart no matter how much he tried to forget her. A stubborn, fascinating woman who would walk to the ends of the earth to find her brother or anyone else she loved. A woman whom he'd tried so hard to erase from his mind.

He shook the thoughts away and focused on the charred remains of the shed.

When the firefighters had been confident the fire would not spark back into life, they'd packed up and rolled away. Now it was up to him to see if there was anything left to save. As he picked his way through the blackened doorway, he puzzled over it again. Had it been dry lightning that started the fire? Or Feria?

Grabbing a rake, he stabbed at the piles of black, unearthing the twisted remains of a drill and two plastic buckets that had melted and fused into a useless lump. He continued to work, pulling and poking at the sooty mess, but retrieved only the bottom of a shovel and a pitchfork that had miraculously survived the blaze. When he emerged from the wreck, filthy and smelling of smoke, he found Anita standing there, scratching Ace behind the ears.

She straightened, wrapped her arms around herself against the chill and gave him a small smile. "I brought more coffee and a sandwich. Is it too early for peanut butter and jelly?"

He managed a laugh. "Never too early for that." Washing his hands under the spigot, he took the sandwich and was surprised to find himself ravenous. He ate and washed it down with hot coffee. "Pops okay?"

She nodded. "He said he had trouble sleeping, but he seems fine this morning. He told me to remind you he's got a doctor's appointment."

Booker started, wiping off his watch to get a look at the time. "I almost forgot."

"I can take him if you'd like."

He looked away from her soft brown eyes that seemed to be filled with pity. "Thanks, but I'll go back and shower and drive him over."

She nodded.

"Any news on Drew?"

Her sigh touched his heart. "Only that Leeman is on a mission to find him. I figure the more people looking the better, but I don't trust Leeman to deliver him to the authorities."

"Yeah. He might just try out his own brand of justice if he gets hold of him." He saw the muscle in her cheek twitch as she clenched her jaw. "Anita, do you have some kind of plan?"

She blinked. "A plan? Why do you ask?"

"Because you have that determined look on your face." *The same one she'd had right before she sabotaged his mine and run away.*

"Just the same plan it's always been—to find my brother."

He eyed her closely. "What can I do to help?"

"Nothing. Really, you've done so much already. You've got your own problems to deal with."

He wanted to move closer, to look deep into her eyes and read what was going on in her soul. "I told you I'd help you find your brother and I will."

She raised her eyes to his but didn't answer. It filled him with an odd sense of fear. She was drifting away again, detaching from his life, as she had last spring.

"I'll see you back at the house later, maybe," she said, as she turned and walked back to the truck.

Even after a long shower, Booker still smelled of smoke as he made his way to the kitchen. He found Pops at the computer, squinting at the screen.

"What are you doing?"

"Building you a Web site."

His mouth fell open. "You're what?"

Pops shot him a look over the top of his half-glasses. "I'm building you a Web site to advertise your touring business. You can't make a go of it unless you have a Web presence."

He felt as though he'd been sucked into a strange, alternate universe. "Where did you learn how to do that?"

"Anita showed me. Not too tricky, really. Easier than fixing a windmill."

Booker could only gape as his father henpecked the keys. "What brought on this desire to learn about computers?"

"I'm going to do something to help around here. Can't just sit around and watch you run yourself ragged. Do you want the 'contact me' box on the main page or just on the 'book a tour' page?"

Still awestruck, Booker marshaled his high-tech father into the Jeep, and they drove into town. On the way, he tried to think of the right way to ask, and finally said, "So, Pops, are you, you know, committed to staying at the ranch?"

His father nodded. "Yes, son. I was born here and I'm meant to die here. I'll try my hardest not to be a burden."

Booker swallowed a lump in his throat. "You'll never be a burden to me."

Pops patted his arm. "I canceled my lease at the assisted-living place."

"You did?" He calculated quickly. That would free up another five hundred dollars a month, which they'd need to put into a new roof. "Great."

"But I'm sorry to tell you, we've got to pay the next three months, anyway, since I broke the lease."

Booker tried to hide his dismay as he drove up in front of the building. "No problem. Just glad to have you back where you belong."

Pops nodded and headed into the physical therapist's office. Booker thought he noticed a spring in his father's step that was worth more to him than any amount of money. He parked and followed Pops in.

The nurse signaled him over. "Your father is such a dear. Everyone here just loves him."

"He does have that effect on people."

She chewed her lip. "Listen, hon. I don't want to have to bring it up, but your bill is due and it's my job to ask about payment."

He nodded. "I remember." He hadn't remembered, fool that he was. Of course the therapist would require payment at some point. "What is, uh, the total on that so far?"

She whispered a figure that took his breath away.

"I see. So what is the due date again?"

Her look was sorrowful. "Well, it's technically due today. I'm sorry to be the bearer of bad news."

"No problem. I'm just going to step out for a minute. Can you tell Pops where I am if he finishes early?"

"Sure."

Booker emerged into the rapidly warming morning, his mind whirling. The shed, the roof, Pops's bills, the broken lease. The final rung in the ladder had broken and he was falling without any way to catch himself.

He couldn't tell them to discontinue Pops's therapy.

He wouldn't let the ranch fold, especially now that his father was coming home to stay.

All his prayers for an easy way out had gone unanswered. There was only one option left.

It was time.

With fingers that had suddenly gone cold, he took out the phone and made the call.

Anita loaded the backpack with a flashlight, a bottle of water and the satellite phone. It was still only a little after noon but she had a feeling, deep down, that tonight would be the night. Ace, who had been busy licking his paws, kept a watchful eye on her. She wondered how Pops had done setting up Booker's new Web site. It made her smile to imagine what Booker's reaction had been at seeing his father hard at work on the computer.

Her heart ached to see the two of them together. It brought back memories of her own father and brother, how close they'd been. For a moment, she considered how things might look now if her parents had lived.

Would she have been so desperate for love that she allowed herself to fall victim to Jack? If she hadn't been sucked into that disastrous relationship, would her heart be open and willing to find another?

Booker's face swam into her mind along with a prayer. *Lord, please help Booker to fight against the forces that are trying to tear his ranch apart. Help him to find the peace and happiness that he deserves.*

With a deep sigh, Anita headed out the door, determined to take another look at the ranch in the daylight before she attempted her nocturnal mission. As she opened the front door, a piece of tattered cardboard fell across the threshold.

Snatching it up, she read the note scrawled there with what looked like a burned bit of wood.

Find me at the equipment shed, route six.

The writing was smeared and indistinct. Was it Drew's? Had he found her and left the message? But why wouldn't he let her know he was there?

Her breath seemed to crystallize painfully in her lungs. Perhaps he'd given Diego the message to deliver. Hands trembling, she looked in every direction for some sort of clue. There was none. The only thing she could surmise was that whoever had left the message did so before Booker returned from his fire watch. Otherwise, Ace would have alerted her to a stranger on the property.

The equipment shed.

She pictured the dark, isolated place where they'd found the message about the overlook, and her skin prickled. She could call Booker on his cell phone and ask him to accompany her. But that would take more time away from his ranch duties. Though she hated to admit it, it would also create alone time for them. Alone time with Booker was the last thing she needed in view of the feelings that threatened to overwhelm her the longer she stayed in the desert.

She should call the police, but she wouldn't, not until she heard from her brother the real truth behind Heidi's death and Leeman's accusations. It was another good reason not to involve Booker. She could not put him in the position of harboring a fugitive, if it came to that.

With shaking hands she grabbed the backpack and an extra bottle of water, plus a small first aid kit she'd bought in town. Whistling for Ace, she climbed into the truck.

The clouds still massed in the distance, their presence pressing the stifling heat back at her as they rolled along Route 6. She prayed she could remember the turn that would take her down to the rusty shed.

What if it's a trap? Her mind played the terrifying scenario over and over. Whoever wanted the camera was after something, some piece of evidence. Would he be waiting inside instead of her brother?

She squeezed the steering wheel as she eased down the last quarter mile and the place came into view. Ace panted at her side, ears pricked, eyes alert. His presence comforted her. If there was an assailant hiding in the shadows, he'd have to get through Ace first.

She parked the truck far enough away from the old structure that the noise wouldn't alert whoever was inside. Easing the truck door open and closed, she left the vehicle and tiptoed over the red earth. With everything inside her, she hoped and prayed it would be her brother this time. If she could just find him, rescue him, all the ugliness would go away. Her teeth clenched as she neared the door, Ace padding along next to her.

Fingers clammy, she pulled the door handle, hauling it open no more than a foot. Ace looked at her as if to say, *Why would you want to go in there?*

She tried to control her chattering teeth. Though her mind screamed at her to stay away, the thought of her brother drove her onward. As quietly as possible, she stepped inside. Ace followed, immediately setting off to explore every corner of the dark space.

Allowing her eyes to adjust to the dimness, she crouched down next to a massive wooden spool and listened.

Silence.

The place felt empty, lifeless.

When Ace returned to her side, she knew it was true. If there had been anyone in the shed, Ace would have sniffed him or her out in a moment. In spite of her sinking spirit, Anita forced herself to her feet and examined the piles of junk, looking for something, anything, to indicate her brother had been there.

The space was messier than she remembered. She wondered

if the disarray was the result of the police search. Or had someone else gone through it? Still searching? Still desperate? A mixture of relief and despair threatened to overwhelm her.

He was not here. Another dead end. The pain of it stabbed her like an ice pick. He was not here, but neither had she found him dead or gravely wounded. She forced herself to exhale and release the tension in her belly.

Someone had wanted her to come. Why? There was nothing here to find, nothing that hadn't already been meticulously gone over.

The realization sizzled through her. It wasn't that someone wanted her to come here. It was a ruse to get her away from the ranch.

"Come on, Ace," she yelled, as she ran to the truck. In a shower of gravel, she slammed the truck into Drive and shot up the bumpy road.

NINETEEN

Anita, you're such an idiot, she berated herself, as she pushed the truck faster on the sizzling road. Sweat beaded on her forehead in spite of the cold fear inside her. She'd blindly gone along with the note, leaving Booker's ranch wide open.

To what? To whom? She hadn't any idea, but panic continued to push her on. Would she find the place on fire? Torn apart?

She had to make it there in time to catch the person in the act, and then she would be able to find her brother. She was sure of it.

The truck crested the steep grade and lurched onto the main road. She thought about dialing Booker's cell and filling him in, but she didn't dare take her hands off the wheel. A car heading in the opposite direction honked at her, the driver shouting at her to slow down.

She continued to race across the molten road, excitement rising inside with each passing mile.

Booker's ranch came into sight in the distance. She was relieved to notice no smoke billowing over the property. A frightening thought occurred to her. What if Pops's appointment had been cut short? Suppose he and Booker had returned home and been surprised by the same person who lured her away?

The thought of something happening to either one of them made her push the truck even faster. They would not suffer anymore because of her or Drew, not if she had anything to say about it.

There was no sign of the Jeep as Anita hurtled onto the property. No sign, either, of any strange vehicle. She pulled up next to the cabin and let Ace out of the truck. He took off like a shot toward the small structure.

She followed after him at a run until she noticed one pertinent fact that stopped her in her tracks. The door to the cabin, the one she'd made sure to lock before she'd left, was ajar.

Booker closed the phone. He was suddenly dead tired, as if the life had been drained out of him. What had he just done?

There were no more options. You didn't have a choice.

The thought didn't console him as he retrieved Pops and paid the physical therapist's bill. He tried not to grimace as he handed over his credit card.

Out in the parking lot, a police car drove in next to them as he finished helping his father into the passenger seat.

Sergeant Williams rolled down the window. "Got a call from Anita Teel. She says someone broke into the guest cabin at your place."

His heart thundered. "Is she…?"

"She's fine. Had the good sense not to go in. Called us first. I'm on my way over there. Care to follow?"

He nodded and dove into the Jeep. Sergeant Williams headed for the ranch. Booker followed.

A break-in? *Feria,* he thought immediately. *Got impatient and decided to send another message.*

You're getting what you want, Feria. Isn't that enough?

He felt his father's eyes on him.

Pops raised a brow. "Tell me what I should be worrying about here."

He shrugged and kept his eyes on the road.

Pops drummed his fingers on his lap. "Why would someone break into our place? Not much to steal there."

He could not tell his father about the terrible decision he'd been struggling with. It was too heavy a burden for an old man. "Don't know. Could be something to do with Drew Teel's disappearance."

"Could be, I suppose. Or maybe not."

He could hear the suspicion in his father's voice. *I'm handling things, Pops. The only way I can.*

They were both silent as they shot across the highway after Sergeant Williams. The important thing was Anita wasn't hurt, he told himself. But would she stay that way? Would Pops? He had to make sure Feria knew of his decision.

The disgust roiled inside him again. He was a rancher, an honest man trying to make a living on land that had been in his family for years. Pops had never been forced to make deals. He wouldn't have allowed the situation to occur in the first place. He'd have kept Feria away with a shotgun if he had to.

Booker bit back a sigh. It was done and there was no use crying about it now.

They parked behind Williams's car. Booker joined Anita and the officer, Pops making his way over more slowly.

"Any sign of the intruder?" Williams asked.

Anita shook her head.

"Stay here until I call you." The officer pulled her gun from the holster and headed inside. Pops took Ace in the house to keep him out of the way.

Booker looked closely at Anita. He could see a lingering fear in her eyes but something else, too. "Where were you when they broke in?"

She flushed slightly and pointed to a piece of cardboard with the note scrawled on it. "I fell for it. I thought it was from my brother."

He wanted to shout at her, to shake her for the pure foolishness of her actions. Hadn't she realized she could have been hurt? Or worse? Thinking of her alone in the isolated place they'd found Drew's makeshift camp sent a chill up his spine. But something about the look deep down in her eyes stopped him from berating her. Instead he pulled her close and pressed a kiss to her temple. "I'm glad you're okay."

She relaxed there for a moment. He felt her body meld against his before she pulled away. "I was stupid."

"No, you were trying to help your brother. That's not stupid. Rash, maybe, but not stupid."

They waited in relative silence until two more cops had come and gone and Williams gestured them in. "I took some initial pictures and dusted for prints in a few obvious places. Didn't find any. I doubt whoever this was left much evidence behind. You can go on in. I'm going to make a call."

Booker and Anita made their way into the cabin. The small window next to the front door had been smashed with a rock, allowing the perpetrator to put a hand through and unlock the door.

Couch cushions were tossed onto the floor, kitchen drawers emptied and the contents of Anita's travel bag strewn about. The furniture was upended. The only thing that seemed to be right side up was Anita's laptop. It lay open on the kitchen table, in sleep mode.

She walked to it and perused the screen. "Someone went through my files and e-mail. Probably looking for something from my brother, I'll bet." She slammed a hand onto the table. "If only I could get a message from him, anything, to let me know he's okay. The unknown is killing me."

Booker sighed. Part of him was relieved the break-in was related to Anita's brother and not his other problem, but seeing the agony on her face was unbearable. "The good news is whoever this is seems pretty convinced your brother is still alive."

"Or they're afraid whatever Drew has may come to light when his body—" She broke off. "I'm going to clean up this mess."

"I'll help."

He fetched a broom and dustpan while she started to work putting the kitchen back in order. The glass lay in jagged bits around the broken window. He swept it up. Pops brought a section of cardboard he'd gotten from the house, and Booker cut a piece to fit over the glass.

Pops then brought them bottles of water from the house. "I'll go find someone to fix this window."

Booker couldn't resist a smile. "Going to look that up online?"

Pops grinned. "Nah, I thought I'd do it the old-fashioned way. With the yellow pages."

Booker saw a tiny smile on Anita's face. "Thanks for giving Pops computer lessons. He's happy to have something to wrap his mind around."

"No problem. I don't know much, but I've helped set up a Web site or two for some of our research teams. Anything more technical than that and you'll need to recruit better help."

He was in the process of fitting the cardboard over the shattered window when his fingers slipped and he sliced his palm. Pulling his hand away, he found the cut to be long, but not deep.

Anita looked up, grabbed a clean towel and hurried over. She guided him down onto a kitchen chair and pressed the cloth on the cut. "Is it bad?"

He looked at her face, etched with concern, and it transported him back to the previous spring. He'd loved her and the moment he got up the courage to tell her, she'd run. Whatever emotion she'd felt for him wasn't enough to keep her there. Maybe he had misread the situation completely. But wasn't it love or at least affection in her brown eyes as she fussed over him now?

She must have felt his stare. Her cheeks pinked and she peeked under the towel. "There is a lot of blood. You might need stitches."

He circled her hand in his. "No, no stitches."

"I forgot. Booker Scott does not require medical attention."

He laughed. "But I tolerate it if it comes from a lovely lady." He pulled her closer. "I can tolerate anything as long as I know you're safe."

She was so close now, he could see the tears collect in the corners of her eyes.

"I'm sorry," she whispered. "That I let this happen. It was so dumb."

Was she talking about the break-in? Or something else? "Don't be sorry. I'm not."

Her fingers danced along his hand as she played with the towel. "I think the bleeding has stopped. I'll get a bandage from the first aid kit."

He forced himself to let her go. When she returned she was more composed, putting a gauze square to the wound and wrapping a strip of bandage around it securely. "That should do it."

He thought about the opal hidden away in his room. It would look perfect hanging around her neck. Would he ever have the courage to give it to her? And would she run away again and take his heart with her once more?

She looked up from her first aid duties. "You have a faraway look on your face."

"I was remembering the springtime."

She colored. "Oh. Yes, I think about that often, too."

"You do?"

She nodded.

Suddenly the need to know overwhelmed him. He took hold of her wrists and brought one gently to his lips, feeling the pulse that throbbed there. "Anita, tell me what happened to us then."

She tried to pull away, but he didn't let her.

"You know what happened. I was trying to save the bats and I apologized for the way I went about it already."

"Forget the bats. I'm talking about us. We were so close, so connected. I showed you every part of my life. I even introduced you to my father. I couldn't think about anyone but you. I was so sure you felt the same. And then, it all changed. Something inside you changed. What was it?" He felt her hands begin to tremble in his.

"Booker…" She pulled her hands away. "It was a mistake for me to let things get to that point between us. I should have learned from my past mistakes." She retreated to the kitchen and fiddled with piles of cutlery.

He followed. "What mistakes? Tell me why you ran away."

"I can't."

"Why not?"

She looked at him. "I can't because I'm not going to let us get that close again. Don't you see? I'm going to leave here just as soon as I can find my brother. I shouldn't have come to stay on your ranch. It wasn't fair of me. I'll make arrangements to return to the hotel tomorrow."

"You don't have to do that."

"Yes, I do. As a matter of fact, I'll call them right now." She tried to pass him.

Without thinking he stepped closer, pulling her to him, so close his lips were inches from hers. He could feel the trembling in her body, the emotion that streamed across her face. "Anita, you still haven't told me why you left."

He heard her breath catch.

"I left because I didn't want to love you." Her voice dropped down to a whisper. "And I don't want to now."

Against every instinct in his being, he let her go.

TWENTY

It took them another hour to clean the place up. Pops arranged for the window repair, then they all shared a simple dinner in the main house. The ransacking unsettled Anita, but the run-in with Booker left her nerves frayed. Her mind lingered on his face, his voice, his touch and she knew she was falling into the same frightening place she narrowly escaped before.

You told him the truth. You can't afford to love him. You've got to find Drew and get away before your heart betrays you again.

Though there had been enough vacancies at the hotel for her to go that night, she stalled, booking for the next morning and praying she'd be able to make her move before she had to leave.

The hours passed slowly, and her plans to keep a steady watch were frustrated at Booker's insistence that Ace stay in the cabin with her.

"I'll keep a close eye out tonight, but nobody gets by Ace."

"Really, it's not necessary. He keeps me awake…with his snoring. I didn't want to mention it before."

Ace gave her an accusatory look, and she made a mental note to find a bone for him.

Booker looked dubious. "I never heard him snore, but if you're really set on that, I'll keep him with me."

"Great," she said, biting back a sigh of relief. Ace would complicate her mission, which was already nearly impossible as it was. "I'm going to turn in for the night." She kissed Pops and headed out, Booker following her to the porch.

"You sure you'll be okay out there?"

The words floated back to her.

The desert comes alive at night.

She was glad the darkness hid her face. "I certainly hope so."

The moon was only a tiny sliver against the cloudy blackness in the hours after midnight. Anita had drunk three cups of coffee in an effort to stay vigilant. Even so, her eyes were heavy as she leaned against the tiny window in the bedroom.

Come on, come on. Where are you?

The ranch remained stubbornly dark. She knew with a cold, hard certainty that she had only one chance to save her brother and this was it. Every hour brought him closer to death out there with no medical care and probably few supplies. She couldn't find him in such a vast landscape, she'd finally admitted to herself, and the person who could might have already killed him.

With a shudder, she checked the backpack again, thankful she hadn't left it behind earlier in the cabin to be searched or stolen by the intruder. The SAT phone was safe, and if her prayers were answered, it would be the lifeline that brought her brother home.

She was in mid-yawn when she saw it. Suddenly every nerve was on fire as she strained to spot it again. There it was, a light bobbing in and out of view.

Feria.

She walked swiftly through the dark house, careful not to crash into any furniture. Easing the door open, she stepped out into the cold night. Immediately she stopped, listening for the sound of Ace's paws skittering over the ground. If he was out on patrol, she'd be hard-pressed to lose him.

The dog didn't come running.

Surprised, she ventured out a few steps farther. When there was still no sound of charging dog feet, she tightened the straps on her backpack, gripped the flashlight and headed off into the night.

The ground was fairly flat before it dropped down into the distant canyon. She tried to keep under the cover of the cotton-wood trees as she crept along. If Feria spotted her from a distance, he might disappear before she could catch up with him. Then again, she thought, he might just shoot her. She remembered the glitter in his eyes when he'd pressed the knife to her throat. If Booker hadn't come along, would he have murdered her? Would he take the opportunity now when she presented herself to him like a trussed turkey ready for the roaster?

Courage, Anita. A cold wind rattled along the ground, carrying with it a myriad of strange noises. She recognized the throaty call of a coyote. A minute later came the answering cry. Coyotes were uninterested in people, she reminded herself. She hoped these coyotes went with the program.

The ground was uneven in places, but she didn't dare switch on the flashlight. She recalled her father's enthusiastic efforts to take his family tent camping.

"Turn off your lights," he'd said. "Let your eyes adjust to the darkness. God will light your way if you trust Him."

I'm trusting You now, God. Give me the courage to do this for my brother. Her foot caught in a crack in the soil, causing her to stumble. She fell, scraping both her palms. When she righted herself, she could no longer see the mysterious lights that had brought her out into the ink-dark night.

Pulse hammering, she stood with her eyes fixed ahead. The lights did not reappear.

Don't panic. They've headed down into the gorge. You can't see them from here. You've got to get closer.

Foot by foot she groped her way nearer to the boulder-strewn canyon. As she moved, she tried to visualize it in her mind. The smugglers hid themselves deep in the folds of rock, winding their way through the canyon as it cut through both Booker's and Leeman's properties. Booker told her the canyon dumped out in a wild area, accessible only by rugged four-wheel-drive vehicles. There the product would be loaded onto trucks and disappear to other distribution points. The terrain and the unwillingness of private landowners to get involved had stalled any law-enforcement efforts to cut off the route.

Something scuttled across the ground near Anita's feet. She almost screamed but instead clapped her hands over her mouth. The scorpion, babies on her back, did not give her even a cursory glance as it continued on its insect mission.

Anita shivered, glad she was wearing sturdy boots and long pants.

She remembered the comforting sound of many wings fluttering through the night in search of insects. Even in her distracted condition, she was pleased to know that somewhere on this ranch a family of bats was darting and zooming through the sky. She itched to record their chittering as they swooped in a great undulating wave. When they were finished, they would fly together back to their roost. Together. A family.

For some strange reason, it was Booker's face that she saw then in her mind's eye. But he was not family; he was helping her, that was all. It was not love, just friendship. But what was that shining deep in his eyes when he looked at her?

Probably the same thing she'd mistaken for love in Jack.

No, Anita. Family is someone who will walk through fire with you, who would never betray you, even in death.

She felt a stabbing pain in her gut. Did she have a family left? Mom and Dad were gone, and with every passing hour the chances of saving Drew diminished. What chance did he have if the only person who could find him was a murderous criminal?

She pushed away the fear. Murderous criminal or not, Feria was going to help her. She quickened her pace, nearly crying out in surprise when she saw a horse tied to a tree in the distance. Unwilling to go nearer, she could only speculate on who it belonged to. Surely Feria and his men wouldn't leave a horse here. She put the thought aside and kept moving.

At the edge of the canyon, she hunkered down low and began her descent along the rocky trail. The smugglers would be alert, she knew, listening for the sound of intruders, ready to deal with any interference.

Her mouth went dry but she forced her feet to move along. Once again she caught sight of the lights fifty yards away. Faintly came the sound of quiet conversation and the low whinny of a horse. She continued to inch ahead, clenching her jaw to still her chattering teeth.

Ahead the path dropped steeply. Anita sidled in next to a massive boulder, hoping not to surprise any animals foraging for a nighttime meal. Fingers pressed to the sandy rock, she eased forward until she could get a look at the path below.

For a moment, she simply did not believe what her eyes told her.

Feria was there with three other men, horses and a heavily laden mule. They stood in the lantern light talking to another man, a tall man with wide shoulders and a dog that paced uneasily around his booted feet.

Booker.

What was he doing here?

She watched with mounting horror as the conversation continued, wishing she dared creep closer to listen in. Booker's arms were folded across his chest, and he listened intently to Feria.

After a moment, Feria gestured to one of his men, who brought forward a metal briefcase. Laying it on a rock, Feria's man opened it.

Anita gasped at the sight of the neat stacks of bills. The surprise caused her to shift her weight and a rock came loose and rolled down the slope.

She froze as all five men turned to look toward the spot where she was concealed.

What was worse, Ace swiveled his furry head in Anita's direction and trotted toward her.

* * *

Booker looked up at the noise.

Feria's eyes narrowed. "You wouldn't have been foolish enough to bring the police with you?"

He almost laughed. "I'm not interested in getting myself shot, thanks. I figured it was another of your guys with a gun trained on the back of my head."

Feria smiled. "If we choose to kill you, you will have the pleasure of seeing it coming, I assure you. Betrayal will not be tolerated."

Booker watched Ace disappear into the rocks. "If there's anyone there, the dog will find them."

Feria nodded to his companion, who closed the briefcase and handed it to Booker. "Then our business is concluded. I will expect no further intrusion on your part."

"And I'll expect none from you. No fires on my property."

Feria raised an eyebrow. "Fires? What would I have to do with that?"

Booker bit back the rage. "You didn't set my shed on fire?"

"Perhaps, perhaps not. It is of no consequence now."

"It's of consequence to me. Now that we've made a deal, my ranch is off-limits. You stay away from my home and my family."

A wind ruffled Feria's hair as he took off his hat. "Does that include your girlfriend? The scientist? She is staying on your property, is she not?"

His gut tightened. Feria had been watching, seeing everything and everyone. He should have guessed the smuggler would carefully investigate anyone before he paid them off. "You've got no business with her."

"True, but her brother has upset the balance in my desert. The police and Border Patrol are asking questions, looking into corners where I do not wish them to look, creating difficulties for me. We operate here—" he gestured to the canyon "—because it is remote, free of complications, you understand."

He forced himself to keep his voice level. "Drew will be found soon. Nothing about his case impacts you—unless you know where he is."

Feria's eyes glittered in the lamplight. "I have not decided what to do about that situation. Where there is much attention, there would be much investigation after a corpse is found. That could prove to be an unfortunate turn of events. Were it not for that consideration, I would have dealt with him already."

"So you do know where he is?"

"Perhaps. I have the matter under advisement. That is all you need to know."

Booker wanted nothing more than to wipe the smug look off Feria's face. There would be no more information gotten from this lowlife.

The injustice of it burned at Booker like acid. How had he gotten here? Taking money from a drug dealer who potentially held Drew's life in his hands? Accepting a bribe from a man who could murder Anita without a pang? Where had it all gone bad?

The money in front of him was enough to save his ranch and get Pops the best therapy available. He could buy solar panels and replenish the herd. The answers to all his problems lay in that briefcase and he took solace in none of it.

He turned his face away. Ace had not returned, but neither had he barked a warning.

Feria adjusted the pack on his horse. "Your dog?"

"If he found someone, you'd know it."

With a graceful step up, Feria mounted the animal. "Then we are done here. I have a schedule to keep."

Booker waited for Feria and his men to depart, not willing to turn his back on the smugglers. He gritted his teeth and picked up the briefcase. When they'd moved down the trail, he turned and whistled for Ace.

The dog didn't reappear.

"Ace," he called. "Let's go."

When there was no response, he yelled again, louder.

After another moment, the dog bounded from behind the rocks, tail wagging.

"Thought you were supposed to be my backup. Nice time to go chase mice."

The dog merely wagged his tail.

"Come on." The trail seemed steeper than it had on the way down. Fatigue pressed on him with a heavy weight. As he passed a massive pile of boulders, Ace grew excited, whining and dancing up and down.

"No more off-roading, Ace. Come." The dog dutifully fell in behind. As Booker passed the rock, he felt a tingle as if someone was watching. He strained his eyes in the darkness but could not see anything in the shadows. With a sigh, he trudged up the trail and mounted the horse.

When the ranch came into view, he was relieved to see both the main house and the cabin were dark. He'd managed to sneak out without waking Pops or Anita. Pulling the horse to a stop, he took it all in. The wide space, dotted with trees older than he was, the windmill turning slowly in the distance, struck him as particularly beautiful. Was it worth the deal he'd made for it?

He passed by the split-rail fence that his father and grandfather had labored on and the well. It had been dug when he was a small boy, but still he could remember the excitement when the men had broken through the hard dry earth and found the precious water. A gift from God, Pops would say.

He wondered what Pops would think about his decision. In a way, it would have been a relief to share it with him or Anita, to lay down the burden for a moment that had hung heavy on his soul since the idea was presented to him.

No, the awful choice was his to bear. His to live with, or die with. He would not ask anyone to help shoulder it.

He thought then of Anita, brown eyes sparkling, hair dancing in the wind. She would be gone soon, he knew. The thought sent his heart plummeting further.

At least there was one thing to be grateful for; she had not been there to see his moment of shame.

After a quick check of the grounds, he stabled the horse and made his way into the house.

TWENTY-ONE

Anita used every bit of ingenuity she could muster to calm Ace when he bounded over to find her hidden behind the boulder. She soothed him, stroked his ears and whispered in a desperate attempt to keep him from barking her location.

It took her mind off the horrible discovery that Booker had made a deal with Feria and come away with a suitcase full of money. She felt sick inside, sick like she had when she'd learned the truth about Jack.

"Quiet, Ace. Don't give me away, boy. Please."

Ace finally trotted off when Booker called the second time. As they trudged by, she thought for one terrifying moment Ace would run back to her. Instead he contented himself with a tail wag and followed his master up over the top of the gorge.

She sat there for what seemed like a long while, willing her legs to stop shaking. They finally did, but the anguish she felt inside did not abate.

Wiping away the tears that trickled down her face, she berated herself. *Why do you care what Booker does? You don't love him, right? You planned all along to leave at the first opportunity. So what does it matter? Go save your brother.*

She forced herself out of her hiding place and followed the sound of the smugglers, who had quietly moved on. The night was colder now, and the thin air seemed to amplify every tiny sound. Creeping as quickly as she dared, she followed the trail, not courageous enough to turn on her flashlight.

It might have been a twisted root or a rock that caught the edge of her foot. She pitched forward and, unable to stop her momentum, tumbled down the steep path until she fell into blackness.

She opened her eyes to find Feria looking down at her. There was no humor or warmth on his face. A mild curiosity was the only emotion she could detect as she gingerly sat up. Feria's men swam into her vision; one had a hand on the gun fastened at his belt.

Feria stared for a moment longer before he spoke. "You are the woman that I met before. What are you doing here? Were you spying for Booker?"

Anita took a deep shuddering breath. "No, I didn't know you were meeting with him. He's no concern of mine. I am looking for my brother and I need your help."

His eyes widened a fraction. "And why is it that you think I could help you in this matter?"

"You said yourself that you know every inch of this desert. I heard from…" She thought about what might happen to Diego if she revealed his identity to this ruthless man. "I heard from someone that you know where my brother is hiding."

"You heard this from whom?"

"It's not important."

His mouth turned up at the corner. "Your situation is not clear to you. I can easily persuade you to tell me anything I want to know."

She forced her chin up. "Yes, I'm sure you can. I'm sure you could also kill me and take me somewhere I'd never be found. It's a risk I'm willing to take because I want my brother back. That's it. That's my motive, pure and simple. You can help me, if you want to."

"And why would I want to do that?"

"I have some money."

He laughed, soft and low. "And so do I."

"I heard some of what you said to Booker. You want my brother's situation resolved to get the cops and Border Patrol to back off, don't you?"

He didn't answer.

"So help me find him and they all go away."

"It might be easier to kill your brother. He's hurt already, isolated. To end things would not be difficult. I have been considering just such a thing, in point of fact."

A wave of terror washed over her, but she shoved it down. "If you kill him, there will be more questions. And if you make me disappear, too, this place will be crawling with cops." She held her breath while Feria considered.

He cocked his head. "I assume you have a plan in mind?"

She nodded, easing the backpack from her shoulder. "Just give him this satellite phone. That's it. I'll take care of the rest."

He took the phone from her trembling hands. "Ms. Teel, I will do this one thing, but that is all. If either one of you implicates me or this turns out to be a trap, there will be no more chances. Do you understand?"

She stared into his hard black eyes. "Yes, I understand."

He nodded once more and joined his men to continue their passage through the canyon.

Anita had to sit after they left to quell a sudden dizziness. She'd done it and he hadn't killed her. The hope surged inside. Drew would call and she would rescue him, without cops, without Border Patrol.

Without Booker.

She thought she'd known him.

How could she have been so wrong?

As the stars glittered overhead, she did not stop the tears this time.

Booker spent a restless night. Feria's face burned at his memory, the man who got what he wanted through fear and intimidation. He thought about the kid in school, twice his size, who regularly knocked Booker over on the way to class. Every time, small as he was, Booker had tried to defend himself only to get punched in the nose.

Then one day, when he was big enough, he'd pinned that boy to the wall, looking at him eye to eye. "Don't," was all he said. The boy never touched him again.

He wished desperately it was that easy now. He was out-manned, outgunned and out of options. The bed was made, so to speak, and now all that was left was to lie in it. His pacing brought him to the dresser drawer. He took out the fiery opal and thought of Anita. If things went bad with Feria, and there was a plenty good chance they would, she could be caught in the cross fire.

No, it was better that she was leaving. He fingered the smooth stone. Could he hide his feelings away again, amid the shirts and socks, allowing her to go without telling her the truth? He'd lost so much already. How much more could he stand? Letting his heart make the call, he slipped the small box into his pocket.

He found Pops settled in at the computer just after sunrise. "Still working on that Web site?"

"Some." His father's forehead creased into a deep frown. "Mostly I've been wondering about something."

"What?"

He shook his head. "Never mind. I'm a nosy old man. Should mind my own beans. Where's Anita?"

"I don't know. She might be busy packing. I'll go check on her."

Pops looked contemplative. "She's going back to the hotel, huh?"

He nodded.

"Gonna just let her go?"

"Yes, sir. She wants to leave, just like she did last time."

"I'm not so sure about that, son."

And I'm not sure about anything anymore, Booker thought, as he made his way to the cabin.

The brilliant morning sunshine was overwhelmed by a roiling mass of clouds. The air felt thick and heavy, filled with the promise of a storm. It seemed the perfect reflection of how he felt on the inside.

Forcing a neutral expression, he knocked on the cabin door.

Anita answered, her face guarded, eyes shadowed with fatigue. "Good morning."

"Good morning. I thought I'd come and see if you wanted breakfast."

"No, thank you. I'm going to pack up and head over to the hotel in a little while."

"I'll drive you."

She shook her head. "No need. I can take the loaner truck and you can pick it up later."

"I've got to return it today, so it would be fine to take you to town. I need to check on a bridle that's being repaired in town, anyway."

She wound a finger nervously in her hair. "Oh, well I guess if that's better for you."

He shifted uneasily. "Anita, is everything okay? You seem worried."

Her smile looked forced. "No more worried than usual. Everything's fine, or it will be when I find my brother."

"New developments?"

"Um, no. No. I just feel like something is going to break soon." She stepped back. "I've got to finish now. Thanks for checking on me. Bye."

Though he didn't pursue her further, his uneasy feeling increased as the morning wore on with no sign of Anita. She hadn't even come in for a cup of coffee. What was she hiding? he wondered. Had she heard from her brother and made plans to meet him?

He promised himself that she would not leave again until he'd said what had burned in his heart for what seemed like forever.

* * *

Anita emerged after lunchtime, bag in hand, which she loaded into the truck. She kept her phone in her purse. There had been no word from Drew, but she knew it might take Feria a while to make contact with him, if he did make good on his promise. She said goodbye to Pops, who was deeply engrossed in the computer.

He gave her a gentle hug. "I hope you won't be a stranger now. Who will give me more computer lessons?"

She saw in his eyes that he understood she did not plan to return. The thought pained her, especially when she imagined what Booker's alliance with Feria would do to the old man.

"You've been so good to me," she said. "I'll miss you." She kissed him on the cheek and left before the tears came.

A hot rain started to fall as she scurried to the truck. Booker was firmly planted in the driver's seat, the wipers already going. He sent an eager Ace back to the house. "Can't ride in the back, boy. Another summer storm coming."

The dog watched dejectedly as they headed down the drive.

As they made their way toward town, Booker shifted. "I wish you'd reconsider staying at the cabin."

She shook her head. "It's time to be a big girl and take care of things myself."

He looked puzzled. "Has something changed that I don't know about?"

Had something changed? Anita almost laughed. *Yes, Booker. Things changed the moment I saw you again. All the strange, frightening feelings opened up and now that you're partners with Feria, I know I'm doing the right thing by running as far away as I can get.* "It's better this way."

She saw his brow furrow and felt again the pain at leaving. This time there would be no coming back. This time, she was saying goodbye to him forever.

They covered the miles in silence. When they arrived at the hotel, the clouds had collected in a dark, unforgiving mass, but no rain had fallen. Booker retrieved her bag from the truck while she checked in. He followed her to her room and waited while she slid the key card in the door.

"Thanks for the lift. I appreciate it, and everything you've done." She turned to go when he caught her arm.

"No. Not this time."

She found herself staring into his blue eyes. "Booker—"

"This time, we finish things once and for all before you run. Tell me what's going on. You owe me that much, Anita."

She desperately tried to think of something to say when she was stopped by a sound that took her breath away. From inside her purse, her phone rang. She froze.

Booker looked at her bag. "Are you going to answer that?"

She wanted to run inside and slam the door, to snatch up the phone and hear what she'd been praying for in the safety of solitude, but she could not risk missing this call. With scrambling fingers, she grabbed the phone.

"Hello?"

Her stomach constricted and the bottom seemed to fall out. It was a voice she would know anywhere. Tears started in her eyes and ran down her face. "Drew. I can't believe it."

Booker eased the door open and pushed Anita gently inside. He waited by the threshold, water streaming down his jacket onto the carpeted floor. She didn't care if he heard, didn't care about anything but that faint voice.

"Are you okay? Tell me where you are?"

Drew coughed and groaned softly, his voice strangely distorted. "Not doing too great. Ran out of food. Think my ribs are broken."

"Drew, tell me where you are right now and I'll come get you. Please."

His voice was so faint she could hardly make out the words. "Mexicans."

She heard a scuffling as though he was losing his grip on

the phone. "I can't understand. Tell me where you are, please. I've got to help you."

"Love you, Ani. Sorry for getting you into all this. Get out of here before he hurts you." His breath sounded loud in the phone, and then the connection clicked off.

"No!" she screamed, phone held so tightly in her hands the knuckles whitened. "No, no, Drew! Don't leave me!" Her cries met with dead air.

Booker pried the phone from her hand and caught her as her knees buckled. He picked her up and carried her to a chair. "What did he say?"

She felt ice-cold, frozen from the inside out. "He's hurt. He told me to leave before I got hurt, too."

"Where is he?"

Frustration nearly left her unable to speak. "All he said was 'Mexicans.' What does that mean?"

He frowned. "I'm not sure."

She hugged herself and rocked back and forth. "He was supposed to tell me where. How can he be gone again? I've got to find him."

"How did he get a phone?"

She jerked as if he'd struck her.

He looked closely into her face. "What did you do, Anita?"

A stream of anger coursed through her, pushing through the fear and frustration. "I met with Feria and asked him to give Drew a phone."

Booker's mouth fell open. "You did what? That's insane. How could you have done that?"

She shot to her feet. "How could *I* have made a deal with Feria? That's pretty hypocritical coming from someone who got a whole briefcase of money from the guy." She saw the shock wash over his face.

"How did you—?"

"It doesn't matter how I know. If you want to partner with a drug dealer, that doesn't concern me. I've got to find my

brother and all I know is he's with a bunch of Mexicans. I—"
The truth sizzled through her like an electric jolt. Her body
filled with an explosion of hope. "I know where he is!"

She grabbed her bag and headed for the door.

Booker stepped in her way, arms folded. "You're not
going alone."

"I don't want you with me."

"I don't care. You're going to get hurt out there."

She tried to push him out of the way. "Leave me alone. I
don't want anything to do with you."

Before she could understand what was happening, he'd
picked her up and thrown her over his shoulder. "This time, it
doesn't matter what you want."

Her desperate wiggles and squirms did nothing to loosen his
grip. Though she beat at his back with her fists, he continued
resolutely outside.

He put her into the truck and got in. Firing up the engine,
he leveled a calm gaze at her.

Fury left her unable to manage a sentence for a moment.
"You are a hardheaded, irritating gorilla of a…cowboy!"

He gave her a smile. "Fair enough. Now, are you going to
tell me where he is, or do we sit here and admire the view?"

TWENTY-TWO

Booker was impressed at how long Anita sat and fumed before she gave him directions to a cave ten miles from the spot where Drew's motorcycle had been found.

"There's a colony of Mexican sheath-tailed bats there Drew helped me photograph," she informed him in clipped tones. "That's what he meant by Mexicans, I'm sure of it."

He drove, eyes riveted to the road, trying to piece together how she'd learned of his meeting with Feria. He should have known it would come out, and the shame left him burning. How could he possibly salvage things now? Stealing a glance at her stony face, he knew he couldn't.

The burning wind increased in intensity until it howled around the truck, knocking and buffeting the sides. He found the mouth of the trail that led to the cave more by luck than anything else. Anita was already out of the truck by the time he'd put it in Park.

Lightning forked the gray sky. The rumble of thunder came next, boiling through the heated air. Underneath their feet the downward-sloping trail was steep in some places and downright precarious in others.

A few minutes into the frantic hike, a sizzle of lightning struck the ground nearby, and Anita screamed. Without another moment's thought, he grabbed her hand and guided them to the shelter of a rocky outcropping. A massive protrusion of red rock screened a bowl-shaped depression in the cliff side, protecting them from the worst.

He sat down on one of the boulders strewn across the space. "Looks like more dry lightning. Best not to be the tallest thing standing around out there."

Anita crossed her arms. "I don't want to stop."

"The worst will pass in a little while."

"My brother is up there, suffering." She whirled on her heel away from him, ready to leave until a crash of lightning outside made her dart back in. He could see the combined fury and frustration on her face.

"Just a few minutes, then we'll head out again," he reassured her.

She sighed loudly and sat on a flat rock, several feet away from him. "Fine. When we find him, I just need you to drive us to the hospital and that's all. Then you're done with the both of us."

He looked at her lovely, angry face and his soul seemed to pour itself into his mouth, pushing past the fear and pride. "I tried to be done with you when you left Rockridge last time, but somehow I can't seem to get you out of my head."

She stared at him, an odd, vulnerable expression stealing over her face. "Why did you do it? Why did you make a deal with Feria?" Her voice dropped to a whisper. "I didn't think you could be that kind of person."

Her words stabbed at him. He took a steadying breath. "You first."

"Me first what?"

"Tell me why you ran away last spring and I'll explain the Feria thing."

She turned away. "No deal."

"Okay then."

They sank into silence. He could see her mind turning it over and over.

Her voice was small when she answered. "Did you... Did you have to do it because of the money?"

He sighed. "This doesn't have anything to do with the mining thing, honey. Don't put it on yourself. It's complicated."

She looked at her feet. "I've been sort of mulling it over in my mind, everything that happened last spring, I mean. I thought I did what I did because I didn't trust you." She hugged herself. "Pops said—he said that I ran because I didn't trust myself."

He spoke gently, feeling she might shatter at any moment. "Pops is real smart that way."

She looked at him then, brown eyes filled with pain that took his breath away. "In grad school, I trusted the wrong person. I wanted so badly to be loved, to belong after my parents died. I was lonely and afraid, I started doing things I wasn't comfortable with in order to please him. He…the man I trusted and loved, I thought…slipped a drug in my drink and tried to rape me."

The words hung in the air and kindled a fury in Booker. That someone, anyone, would do such a thing made him want to break things. His fingers clenched into fists. "Anita," was all he could manage.

She waved a hand. "A friend saved me. I thought I'd put the whole thing behind me, but when I came to Rockridge, I guess I started feeling things for you and…I was scared. I shouldn't have allied with Leeman, shouldn't have run away. I know the right thing to do was talk to you about the mine and…everything, but I was afraid that my feelings would betray me and I wouldn't be able to walk away." Her voice trembled. "I guess Pops is right. I don't trust myself."

He couldn't stand it any longer. He walked to her and gathered her into his arms. "I'm so sorry, honey. So sorry that happened to you."

She cried, wrenching sobs muffled by his shirt. He tried to still the shuddering that swept through her, to somehow put into his embrace the storm of feeling that swept through him.

He held her until the grief receded and she looked up, face shining with tears. "I've prayed and prayed for God to help me escape my fears."

He wiped the moisture from her face. "And instead He's helping you face them."

She managed a shaky smile. "I liked my way better."

He laughed. "Good thing God's plan is always better than ours." He reached into his pocket and pulled out the box. "I wanted to give you this in the spring, but I think this is as good a time as any."

She stared at the box for a long while before she opened it. Her eyes widened in wonder as she looked from the opal to him. "Is this from your mine?"

He nodded. "But I promise I didn't startle any bats to get it."

She lifted it from the box, letting the dim light catch the fire in the stone. "Why would you give this to me?"

He inhaled deeply before he spoke. "Because, Anita, I love you." He wanted to say many more things, but he couldn't get the words out.

Her face was a picture of tender emotion. "Booker, I…"

He couldn't take it. The thought of her turning him down was too much. "Here," he said, taking the necklace from her cold hands. "Don't say anything, just wear it. That's enough." He came around behind her, breathing in the warmth of her body, his fingers skimming the soft curve of her neck as he fastened the clasp. Then he kissed her, very gently, at the spot just below her ear. He heard her sigh, a small sound, like the fluttering of bird wings.

The phone in his pocket rang. He grabbed it, grateful for the interruption to his emotional upheaval. "Hey, Pops. Surprised I get cell coverage here. Is everything okay?"

He called Anita over. "Pops says he needs to tell us something." He held the phone so they could both hear.

"I'm a nosy old codger," Pops said, "but I've been thinking about Leeman's birthday boat."

"What?" Booker said, thinking he'd misheard.

"The boat Gershwin was helping Heidi pick out for Leeman's birthday."

Anita frowned. "Why were you thinking about that?"

"Just seemed odd that Heidi would be picking one out for a man she was leaving, doesn't it?"

Booker agreed. "That occurred to me but I didn't give it much more thought. So what did you find out?"

"I've been on this site that auctions boats and I found the *Queen Bee,* the one Gershwin said Heidi was looking at. The thing goes for a hundred fifty thousand dollars and change. Can you beat it?"

Anita gave Booker a "Where is this going?" look. He shrugged.

Pops went on. "Seems the boat was purchased for full asking price."

Anita's eyes widened. "So Heidi really did buy that boat?"

"Not Heidi. Boat was bought by a P. Gershwin. Yesterday."

Anita was so stunned by the information she sank back down on the rock. Paul Gershwin. Suddenly bits of information began to assemble in her mind like pieces in a puzzle. Paul Gershwin had been well apprised of their search for Drew since the day he'd arrived.

She looked up to find Booker staring at her.

"Robin was supposed to have a teleconference with Gershwin the day we went to look at the tortoise grounds. She must have told him we'd be there and he tried to run us off the road."

She nodded. "That's probably how he hurt his shoulder. He's been looking for something Drew's got. That's why he lured me out of the cabin, that's why he's been searching Robin's house under the pretense of planning Heidi's memorial." Her mind raced. "He's always resented working for Leeman. He's never been given his shot at running the magazine."

Booker frowned. "So he did what? Stole money from the business? Had some sort of relationship with Heidi to cover it up?"

Anita's body prickled in horror. "I think he killed her and tried to frame my brother, but there's some piece of evidence he didn't get his hands on, evidence that will prove Gershwin is guilty."

Booker paced the ground. "There's no other way a magazine editor could afford a boat like that."

She wanted to scream. "I never suspected it. I trusted him. I trusted him." Her body began to shake.

Booker took her by the shoulders. "We all trusted him. He's a liar and a murderer and even the cops didn't see it. We've got to go get your brother and get to the police."

She looked into his eyes and wanted with all her heart to believe him. If she could only reach out and take what he offered, leave the fear and doubt behind.

An image of Feria rose in her mind.

He must have read her thoughts. "Anita, I can't take time to explain everything right now, but you've got to trust me. Look at me."

She forced herself to look into the intense blue of his eyes. She tried to speak but nothing came out.

Booker touched her gently on the cheek. "You know I love you and deep down, no matter what things look like, you know what kind of person I am inside. I promise I'll explain it all later, but right now, you've got to trust me. Can you do that?"

She felt so cold inside, as if she stood on the edge of a wind-swept precipice. It was the moment she'd been running from since her parents died, since that awful night with Jack.

Lord, can I trust this man? The words from Romans 8:28 rose inside her heart.

And we know that in all things God works for the good of those who love Him, who have been called according to His purpose.

For the good of those who love Him.

All she could see was those blue eyes. She did not know why Booker made that deal with Feria. She did not understand how he would escape his connection to the drug dealer. But she did know, without question, that Booker loved her and loved God.

It was enough.

Slowly, she held her hand out to his.

* * *

They had waited so long in the rock shelter, what sunlight there was had begun to wane. Booker was relieved to see that the lightning had passed as they picked their way out of the shelter, leaving behind a muggy stillness. He'd taken only a moment to call Pops and direct him to summon the police. Until help arrived, they were on their own.

Anita took Booker's hand as he helped her over a steep cluster of rocks. "I know my brother doesn't want the police involved, but we've got to have enough evidence now to clear his name, don't we?"

Booker didn't say what he was thinking. *We've only got suspicions right now. We'll need some sort of hard evidence to clear his name.* "We had no choice but to involve them at this point. Paul Gershwin has to be stopped before he kills someone else."

The path dropped down into a hollow. They paused for a moment to catch their breath. Booker pointed to a shadowed crevice on a rise a hundred yards above them. "Is that the cave?"

Anita nodded, cheeks flushed from exertion. "He's there. I know he's there. I can feel it."

Booker scanned the terrain all around.

"What are you looking for?"

"Signs that someone found this place before we did."

Her face paled. "Gershwin?"

"He's been keeping a pretty close eye on you. I didn't see anyone following, but it pays to keep an eye out."

They started up the steep incline, trying to keep from slipping on the loose gravel. Anita pushed the hair out of her face. "How would Drew have gotten up here injured?"

"It's amazing what you can do when survival's at stake."

They climbed for another quarter hour until the mouth of the cave was in sight, accentuated by the long rays of light. He turned to her. "Honey, I know you have a lot riding on this, but I just want you to be careful."

Her eyes met his. "In case he's—he's not alive?"

He hated the fear that rekindled in her eyes. "We've tried to call him several times on the SAT phone and still no connection."

Her lips trembled but her chin remained high. She fingered the opal that hung around her neck. "I'll face it, whatever it is."

He wanted more than anything to hold her, to kiss her. It was not the time and, he reminded himself, he'd not heard her say it. His had been the only admission of love today. Ignoring the crush of worry that crowded his chest, he surveyed the landscape one more time before they headed into the cave.

Inside, his senses were overwhelmed, first by the darkness and then by the strong smell of ammonia. The cave was cool, a good ten degrees cooler than the outside air.

Anita breathed in his ear. "The bats are still here. The smell comes from their droppings."

He pressed his face to hers. "Stay here for a minute, let your eyes adjust." Her body was taught, every muscle tensed and ready, but she nodded.

They stood, hand in hand, as their vision accommodated itself to the darkness.

The cave opened into a sort of antechamber, strewn with rocks and red dust. It narrowed into a sort of passageway in the back end, wide enough for two people to pass through abreast. He heard Anita gasp as she bent to snatch an item from the ground.

It was an empty wrapper from a granola bar.

Her eyes locked on his.

"He's here," she breathed. "My brother is here."

TWENTY-THREE

Anita's stomach spasmed as they made their way to the opening at the back of the cave. The ammonia smell was stronger here, but not overwhelming. She stumbled over a rock and Booker caught her arm.

She clung to his hand, grateful to have him by her side. More than grateful, she thought, remembering the wild rush she felt when he admitted he loved her. The knowledge swam around inside her, whipping her mind into a confusion of joy and fear.

Focus on Drew.

Pushing farther into the darkness, she pulled out her flashlight and beamed it into the area ahead. Disappointment flooded through her. He was not there, only darkness and shadow. It wasn't possible. He had to be somewhere in the cave.

"Drew!" she cried out, unable to hold in the despair.

From the back of the cave came a whisper, so low she almost missed it.

"Ani."

She stumbled forward, falling, half screaming as she made it to the prostrate figure almost obscured by shadow. "Drew." Through her tears it was difficult to see him clearly. She rubbed a hand across her eyes and knelt by her brother. His face was bruised and pale. Dried blood on his forehead stood out darkly against his skin.

"Oh, Drew. I can't believe it's you." Grabbing his cold

hand, she breathed prayer after prayer to the Father for delivering him.

Booker hunched next to them, taking out the first aid kit and running his flashlight over Drew's body.

"Is that Booker?" Drew whispered.

Booker patted his shoulder. "You bet. It's been a real adventure trying to find you."

Drew's chapped lips crimped into a faint smile. Anita pressed a bottle of water to his mouth. "We're going to get you out of here. The police are on their way."

She felt him tense. "It's okay. We figured out Paul Gershwin is the reason behind all of this."

He nodded. "The disks in my backpack. He's after them." Drew gestured to Booker to retrieve them. "Gershwin had an affair with Heidi and she discovered he was embezzling. She was afraid to tell her husband, afraid of Gershwin. I offered to help, to go with her to Mexico and get her settled. We arranged to meet." He closed his eyes.

"But Gershwin got there first," Booker offered, as he pulled a box of computer disks from Drew's bag.

Drew nodded. "We struggled and he killed her with my gun. He told me Williams and Rogelio were on the take and nobody would believe I didn't do it. He had everything figured out except the fact that Heidi had already given me the disks and I'd copied them as backup. We struggled and I got away. Not for long. Had to ditch my bike and hide out when he caught up with me. Feria's men found me at the equipment shed so I cleared out of there, too. I figured Gershwin made some sort of deal with Feria to flush me out. Didn't know who to trust."

She thought about Feria and the briefcase. Who to trust? *That's the crux of both our lives at the moment, brother.*

He grabbed Anita's hand. "Never should have involved you, sis. I'm sorry."

She squeezed his fingers. "You're my brother. There's nowhere I'd rather be than right here."

Booker held a flashlight to his watch. "It's going to be sunset in a few minutes."

Drew managed a smile. "Oh, yeah. Don't I know it. This cave is wired to come alive at sunset."

Anita laughed. Now that Drew was safe, she allowed joy to fill her heart again. She plied him with another drink of water. "Can you walk?"

"I can try," Drew said.

"If not, I'll carry you." Booker stood and shouldered both backpacks just as a figure stepped through the mouth of the cave.

It didn't matter that the lantern light blinded them for a moment. Booker knew who was holding the light even before the voice.

"Thanks for finding him. I've been working on that for a solid week." Paul Gershwin lowered the lantern slightly. His face glowed eerily, and a gun shone in his hand.

Drew groaned and Anita shot to her feet. Booker held up a hand to her and tried to step between Anita and Gershwin, but the man waved him off with the gun.

"I'd like to get out of here by dark. It's a rotten climb as it is. I'm sure you've summoned the cops, so I'm going to need to make it look like Drew killed you both." He smiled. "Give me the disks."

Booker's mind raced, looking for a way to save them. "Why would we do that if you're just going to kill us, anyway?"

"Because I can do it the easy way, or the hard way." He waved the gun at Anita. "You don't want your girl to die slowly, do you?"

Booker tried to tamp down on the rage that rose inside him. He glanced at Anita. How could he get her out of this alive? Something in her face riveted him. She was desperately trying to tell him something. He stalled.

"You didn't have to kill Heidi."

He laughed. "Things got out of hand. But to all appearances, I didn't kill her. Drew did. That's what the forensics proved. His gun and all."

"We know the truth, Gershwin." Booker eased a step forward and noticed the tiny movement as Anita tapped her watch and pointed a finger upward. What was she trying to tell him?

Then he got it. A few minutes was all they needed. He wasn't sure it would be enough, but it was the only chance they had. "Why steal at all? You got a nice job. Decent living, enough to put food on the table, right?" He watched Gershwin's face twist in rage.

"I deserve more than a decent living. I've killed myself building up that magazine and Leeman wouldn't give me the recognition I deserved. My father got beaten down by this life, but I won't."

One minute more, tops.

"Going to sail your boat away?"

Gershwin started. "Oh, you figured that out? You're smarter than you look." He cocked the gun. "Enough blabbing. I've got to finish up here."

Booker heard it, the sound of a million rushing wings. "Or not," he said as he dropped to the floor with Anita.

The bats streamed out of the mouth of the cave like a roaring stream, heading into the sunset to feed. Anita heard Gershwin cry out as the leathery wings swept around him. She felt the breeze from their flight whirl through the breadth of the cave. As soon as the rush subsided enough for her to look up, she saw Booker launch himself at Gershwin.

Had Gershwin managed to keep his hold on the gun?

Her question was answered a moment later when a shot deafened them, bouncing off the rock above her head. She threw herself on top of Drew as another shot sailed above and drilled into the cave side.

Booker. A fear greater than anything she'd felt before took hold of her as she watched Booker struggle with Gershwin, tumbling and crashing against the jagged stones.

Fingers cold with terror, she grabbed a rock and ran toward them.

When Gershwin struggled to his feet, she brought the rock down as hard as she could on his head.

He managed to sidestep and the blow caught him on the shoulder. Enraged, he turned toward her, gun aimed at her chest. There was nowhere to hide. All she could do was stare down the muzzle of the gun.

It happened in a blur. Booker leaped in between them as the shot was fired. The blast deafened her and she screamed. Booker hit the ground in a shower of gravel and lay there at her feet, perfectly motionless. Gershwin stared, panting, sweat rolling down his temples.

He smiled. "That takes care of that." He raised the gun again.

Agent Rogelio's voice rang through the cave. "Drop it, Gershwin."

Rogelio climbed into view, gun leveled. Williams was two paces behind him.

With a pained grimace, Gershwin lowered the gun.

Anita dropped to her feet, gently rolling Booker over.

His eyes were closed. She desperately searched his body, finding blood spreading out from his shoulder in a crimson tide. She cried, pressing her face to his. She felt as though she'd come to the end of a long journey that started the day her parents were killed.

All the things she'd learned, the frightening places she'd been, seemed to crystallize, clear and sharp in the gloom of that cave. Jack was behind her, left in another time long ago. This man, lying at her feet, his blood pouring into her hands, this man was the person she should have trusted all along. *Please, God. Please.*

Her tears slid down and wet his face. "Don't leave me, Booker. I love you. Don't leave me, please."

Somewhere in her mental haze she became aware of Agent Rogelio kneeling next to them. He lifted Booker's collar and checked the wound.

"Missed the heart. Looks like he took one in the shoulder. He'll live, the thick-skinned cow jockey."

Booker's eyes opened. He looked into her face. "You okay?"

She laughed, tears running down her chin. "Yes, yes, I'm okay. Drew's okay, too. *You're* the one with the bullet inside you."

Rogelio cleared his throat. "Hey, Scott. Thought you'd like to know the bust is going down tonight."

Booker's eyes widened. "Tonight?" He struggled to get up. "I've got to get Pops out of there."

"Already done. When he called to fill us in on Gershwin, I sent an undercover unit over to pick him up. I heard he's teaching the guys how to set up a Web site." Rogelio laughed. "We've got extra men coming on for the bust tonight. When Feria reaches the wasteland, he's in for a surprise and his transport people, too. Pretty sweet setup, if I do say so myself."

Anita struggled to take it in. "What are you talking about?"

Rogelio stood. "Finally got this stubborn mule to wear a wire, take a bribe from Feria. We taped it all, put a watch on the place and tonight we'll move. We'll bust Feria and his guys and their shipment."

Booker closed his eyes and sighed.

Rogelio chuckled. "Looks like you'll get the twenty-thousand-dollar reward offered for assisting the cops, too. That should build you a new shed."

A wan smile lit Booker's face. "Yeah."

Rogelio left to help Williams haul Gershwin to his feet and out of the cave.

A helmeted firefighter made his way into the cave and began to treat Drew. Another checked Booker's vitals and went to fetch a stretcher.

Anita pressed her face to Booker's. The opal brushed against his cheek.

He cupped it and traced a finger along her lips, an almost shy look coming over his face. "Thought it might be nice to have a matching piece made." He pulled her hand to his cheek and gently touched her left ring finger. "A ring, maybe."

Her heart squeezed at the bare emotion in his expression.

He cleared his throat. "I can't give you much, just a ranch

that's in trouble and a lot of dried-up land and, and my name." He looked at her for an endless moment, the question shimmering in his eyes. "Would that be enough?"

Tears spilling down her cheeks, she gave him a long kiss. When she pulled away, she saw happiness on his face and a deep love that was as wide and endless as the desert itself.

"That is more than enough."

Booker pulled her close again. The love rose inside, filling her and soaring upward like a great rush of wings.

* * * * *

Dear Reader,

The desert is a place of harsh extremes, a wilderness filled with incomparable beauty and deadly hazards. Here Anita Teel finds herself fighting for her brother's life. Lost and hopeless, she struggles to learn to trust herself and God's loving plan for her. Doesn't it seem to you, kind reader, that whether we toil in the arid desert, the bustling big city or a small Midwestern town, our struggles to trust and accept God's love are the same?

Thank you kindly for sharing your time with Anita and Booker. I hope we can all find our strength, as they do, in the words of Romans 8:28.

And we know that in all things God works for the good of those who love Him, who have been called according to His purpose.

I so enjoy hearing from my readers. If you would like to contact me, you can do so via my Web site at www.danamentink.com.

Fondly,

Dana Mentink

QUESTIONS FOR DISCUSSION

1. Anita is proud of her work as a scientist. Does she allow that pride to cause problems in her relationships with others?

2. Booker doesn't want to help Anita initially because of past hurts. Have you ever written someone out of your life because they wronged you?

3. The story takes place in the heart of the Arizona desert. How is this untamed place a metaphor for the human experience?

4. Agent Rogelio says, "I go around with a target painted on my back." In a dangerous, disappointing world, how can we avoid feeling this way?

5. At night, Anita is told the desert "comes alive" with wonders unseen during the daylight hours. What are the wonders in your own region that a visitor might overlook?

6. Gershwin's father killed himself. How does such a terrible event shape the lives of the family left behind?

7. Though Anita has no claim to Booker, she resents his relationship with Robin Hernando. Are her misgivings about Robin reasonable, or merely the product of jealousy?

8. Ace is a faithful canine companion throughout the story, yet he came from an abusive situation. Why is it so common for animals to be neglected or abused in a society with such an abundance of resources?

9. Booker believes Anita is strong and delicate at the same time. How is it possible to be both things?

10. Heidi Leeman is caught between two controlling and violent men. Would she have been able to escape the situation without running? How?

11. Pops tells Anita that she is afraid to trust herself: How can we rely on God to help us face our lack of faith in our own decisions and abilities?

12. What do you think the future will hold for Anita and Booker?

Private investigator Wade Sutton plans to hightail it out
of Dry Creek long before December 25. The town
holds too many *unmerry* memories. Until he's asked to
watch over a woman in danger, a woman whose faith
changes him forever.

Turn the page for a sneak preview of
SILENT NIGHT IN DRY CREEK
by Janet Tronstad
Available in October 2009
from Love Inspired®

Wade wished he had never come back to Dry Creek. Or, since he had come back, he wished people hadn't been so kind to him. Barbara making that cake for him was putting him off his game. And then Jasmine—usually he didn't have any trouble taking a tough line with a suspect. But then, he'd never been tempted to kiss a suspect before.

He watched Jasmine's back as she walked to the table. She was ramrod straight and angry with him. He knew he'd come on too strong, but it was either that or forgetting everything he knew about law enforcement and refusing to believe she could be responsible for anything.

As a lawman he had to consider all the possibilities, and it was hard to forget that Lonnie had been her partner. She could have sent him a coded message that in some way had helped him escape from prison, or at least given him an incentive to risk everything to get outside.

He wished he knew how to look into the heart of a person so he would know what Jasmine was thinking. Was she as innocent as she looked, or as guilty as she had been the first time she was convicted of a crime? He knew better than most how many ex-cons fell back into theft. He was often the one who took them in the second time around and listened to their sorry excuses.

"I gave you the biggest piece of cake," Barbara said as he sat down at his place at the table.

"Thank you." Wade smiled. It was the cake of his childhood fantasies, and he was going to have to force himself to eat it. All he wanted to do was take Jasmine home and then park his car at the end of the lane to her father's place. Why did she have to be tied up with Lonnie? Why couldn't she be a nice, ordinary woman like Barbara here? Carl never had to worry about arresting *her*.

Wade felt the smoothness of the cake on his tongue and the sweet tang of the raspberry filling. He smiled up at Barbara and thanked her again for the cake. The two kids at the table were smacking their lips and demanding more, just as Wade would be doing if he wasn't so troubled.

Then he looked down the table and saw his dear friend Edith. She wouldn't be happy about him keeping an eye on anyone. It was clear the older woman was very fond of Jasmine. That, of course, was the problem with being a lawman and trying to have friends. He liked things black and white with no shades of gray. He didn't want to have feelings for the suspect.

By doing his job, he was going to upset Jasmine and everyone else in Dry Creek. For the first time since he'd driven into town, he missed the barren feel of his apartment in Idaho Falls. He knew who he was there.

It didn't take long for Wade to leave the Walls' house, with Jasmine walking in front of him. The night was cold. Jasmine wrapped her arms around her body to keep warm and hurried to his car. He was still nursing that leg of his, so he went more slowly than she did. He made it in good time, though, and as he opened the car door for her, she nodded her thanks and slid into the passenger seat.

The first thing Wade did after he got into the car was to move the dial up on the heater. Snowflakes were just starting to fall, but they were scattered enough that he could clear them away with his windshield wipers.

He silently turned his car around and started down the sheriff's lane. The car lights shone on the falling snow, making the flakes look like pinpricks in the darkness.

"You don't think Lonnie would do something to my father, do you?" Jasmine asked. She looked up at him with eyes full of worry. "Lonnie's not very stable. I wouldn't want anyone around here to be hurt by him."

Wade shrugged. "With all you'd inherit if Elmer were out of the picture—"

Jasmine gasped. "I don't care about the money."

"Lonnie might."

That turned her quiet. He didn't want her to worry, though.

"He won't even have the chance to get close to anyone," Wade assured her. "We'll have the feds all over the place by tomorrow. Lonnie has a better chance of breaking in to Fort Knox than he has of sneaking into Dry Creek."

Wade hoped he wasn't lying. He had no idea what the feds would do. And they might have some completely different theories as to why Lonnie had broken out of prison. It might have nothing at all to do with Jasmine or anyone in Dry Creek.

"You'll be safe," Wade said as he opened his door.

He walked around to the passenger door and opened it. Wade stood by the open car door and watched as Jasmine pulled her coat closer to her body. She wasn't making any move to walk toward the house and he wasn't making any move to let her. Finally Wade reached out and touched her cheek. It was soft and a little damp. She must have been crying when she'd been huddled against the door on the drive out here.

"It'll be okay," he whispered to her as he brought his hand down.

"I'm fine," she said.

He nodded with a slight smile. "I know."

Wade had never kissed a suspect, but he would have done it now if he hadn't thought it would make Jasmine cry even more. She was barely hanging on, and he needed to leave her with her dignity.

"I'll be parked at the end of Elmer's lane if you need me,"

Wade said as he stepped back from the door. Snow was falling
in earnest now, but in his trunk he had a heavy sleeping bag that
he used on stakeouts like this. "I'll come to the door in the
morning, before I go over to my grandfather's."

"You can't sleep outside all night. It's freezing out here. I'll
leave the kitchen door unlocked in case you need to come inside."

"Don't leave anything unlocked. I'll duck into the barn if
I need to."

Jasmine nodded.

Wade watched her walk to the kitchen door and go inside
the house. Only then did he head back to the driver's door. He
wondered if he'd get any sleep tonight. He was losing his edge.
The next thing he knew, he was going to be offering pillows to
everyone he arrested and wishing them sweet dreams. When
had he turned into a soft touch?

He waited for the light to go out in the kitchen before he
started his drive down the lane. He already felt lonely.

* * * * *

*Will Jasmine give Wade reason to call
Dry Creek home again?
Find out in
SILENT NIGHT IN DRY CREEK
by Janet Tronstad
Available in October 2009
from Love Inspired®*

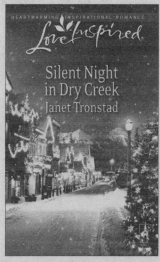

Love Inspired

For private investigator Wade Sutton, Dry Creek holds too many memories—and none of them fond. Yet he can't say no when the sheriff asks him to watch over a woman who might be in danger. Getting to know lovely Jasmine Hunter just might give Wade a good reason to call Dry Creek home once more….

Look for

Silent Night in Dry Creek

by

Janet Tronstad

Available October wherever books are sold.

www.SteepleHill.com

Steeple Hill®

REQUEST YOUR FREE BOOKS!

2 FREE RIVETING INSPIRATIONAL NOVELS
PLUS 2 FREE MYSTERY GIFTS

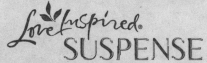

Love Inspired.
SUSPENSE

YES! Please send me 2 FREE Love Inspired® Suspense novels and my 2 FREE mystery gifts (gifts are worth about $10). After receiving them, if I don't wish to receive any more books, I can return the shipping statement marked "cancel". If I don't cancel, I will receive 4 brand-new novels every month and be billed just $4.24 per book in the U.S. or $4.74 per book in Canada. That's a savings of over 20% off the cover price. It's quite a bargain! Shipping and handling is just 50¢ per book.* I understand that accepting the 2 free books and gifts places me under no obligation to buy anything. I can always return a shipment and cancel at any time. Even if I never buy another book, the two free books and gifts are mine to keep forever.   123 IDN EYM2 323 IDN EYNE

Name	(PLEASE PRINT)	
Address		Apt. #
City	State/Prov.	Zip/Postal Code

Signature (if under 18, a parent or guardian must sign)

Mail to Steeple Hill Reader Service:
IN U.S.A.: P.O. Box 1867, Buffalo, NY 14240-1867
IN CANADA: P.O. Box 609, Fort Erie, Ontario L2A 5X3

Not valid to current subscribers of Love Inspired Suspense books.

Want to try two free books from another series?
Call 1-800-873-8635 or visit www.morefreebooks.com

HEARTWARMING INSPIRATIONAL ROMANCE

Get more of the heartwarming inspirational romance stories that you love and cherish, beginning in July with SIX NEW titles, available every month from the Love Inspired® line.

Also look for our other
Love Inspired® genres, including:

Love Inspired® Suspense:
Enjoy four contemporary tales of intrigue and romance every month.

Love Inspired® Historical:
Travel to a different time with two powerful and engaging stories of romance, adventure and faith every month.

Love Inspired®
SUSPENSE

TITLES AVAILABLE NEXT MONTH

Available October 13, 2009

HEARTS IN THE CROSSHAIRS by Susan Page Davis

She came to be inaugurated—and left dodging bullets.
Dave Hutchins of Maine's Executive Protection Unit doesn't
know who wants to kill governor Jillian Goff. Still, he won't
let her get hurt on his watch, not even when he finds his
own heart getting caught in the crosshairs.

GUARDED SECRETS by Leann Harris

"If I die, it won't be an accident." Lilly Burkstrom can't
forget her ex-husband's words...especially after his
"accidental" death. As her fear builds, the only person this
single mother can trust is Detective Jonathan Littledeer.
Can he keep Lilly safe?

TRIAL BY FIRE by Cara Putman

Her mother's house was first. Then her brother's. County
prosecutor Tricia Jamison is sure she's next on the arsonist's
list. But who is after her family? And why does every fire
throw her in the path of Noah Brust, the firefighter who
can't forgive or forget their shared past?

DÉJÀ VU by Jenness Walker

Cole Leighton can barely believe it when a woman on his
bus is abducted—in an *exact* reflection of a scene from the
bestseller he's reading. Someone's bringing the book to life...
and Kenzie Jacobs is trapped in the grisly story. Now the
killer is writing his own ending, and none of the twists and
turns lead to happily ever after.

LISCNMBPA0909